a cautionary tail
and other plays

by christopher oscar peña

NoPassport Press Dreaming the Americas Series

performance rights and inquiries:

management:

Henry Huang
Station 3
1051 N. Cole Ave, Suite B
Los Angeles, CA 90038
310.204.4444
henry@stationthree.com

NoPassport Press Dreaming the Americas Series
Founding editor: Caridad Svich
NoPassportPress@aol.com, www.nopassport.org

ISBN: 978-1-304-63736-9

this collection is dedicated

to my parents **Maribel** and **Oscar Peña**
first, last and always
for giving me a voice

to **Naomi Iizuka, Chay Yew, Anne Garcia-Romero**
and **Luis Alfaro**
for their unwavering support and guidance

and to
Mikaela Feely-Lehmann
and
JD Taylor
for keeping me

and finally for
John Eisner / The Lark Play Development Center and all
who work there

for keeping the lights on

love
it's taken me so long
it's taken me so long
love
it's tearing me apart
it's tearing me apart
and love
I don't even know what for
I don't even know what for

I'm without you

-Without, *My Gold Mask*

Contents

The plays:

acknowledgements

my father recently told me that as a kid the first thing i ever told him i wanted to be when i grew up was a writer. i have no memory of this event whatsoever but there is a sense of pride in his voice when he tells me this. it's as if he's proud of himself for getting out of my way and giving me the room to grow to be anything i wanted. i DO remember saying that when i grew up i wanted to be a doctor. my mom had severe back pain most of my life (oddly enough no doctor could ever pinpoint why) so i remember announcing i would become a doctor so i could cure her. at one point i think i said i would become an astronaut, a laughable occupation when i think of it now, as i have a hard enough time flying on earth, let alone out in the vast universe. i spent a lot of time in bookstores as a child, reading book after book after book, or in the back seat of the family car on family outings. i felt fear and excitement getting lost in other peoples lives, but i also felt comfort. i was lonely then, and somehow, through other peoples stories, i was able to connect to something bigger.

fast forward, years later, to this moment now. many writers complain that the act of writing, that being a writer, is an extremely lonely thing. it is, it can be. i chose to be a playwright because i love the medium. i love the ephemeral beauty of it all. i love the collective breath that an audience shares as something new is revealed. i like that a play is a blueprint for interpretation and that every production (hopefully, there will be many) will be different and bring something completely new and revelatory to the experience. but most of all, i love the people. i love getting up and going to rehearsal and watching a director make sense of words i've written down. i love that moment where an actor reinterprets a line and discovers something so much deeper i didn't know was there. i love the designers who make magic out of the unsolvable. i love going to the theater and standing in the lobby with the staff at intermission and hearing audience members whisper about what they're seeing. i love that moment at an early reading with a small group, where you watch a fellow playwright finally crack that thing they've been wrestling with, excited to run home and tell friends I WAS THERE. i love watching someone try something new, fail, but fail epically. most times, "failing" turns out to be more interesting than "succeeding." i love going to the bar after and arguing about what we've seen, about our shared experiences, about what we might have missed. i just love the people. it is through the theater that i finally found community, that i finally found my tribe. the theater is where i found my second family and where i made something out of my loneliness, made it something more. so i would love to express my deepest gratitude and love to the people, artists and organizations that have made these plays, and this life, possible:

- my mentors for giving me an artistic lineage: Naomi Iizuka (for being the first person to call me a playwright over a decade ago, and for this beautiful intro), Anne Garcia-Romero, Luis Alfaro and Eduardo Machado (and one amazing class with Itamar Moses)

- i have been very lucky to collaborate with some of the most incredible and gifted directors, each rare in their own beautiful way. for the thought provoking questions, the challenges to push deeper, for the hand-holding, late night e-mails, for taking care of me when i was on the verge of tears, for dinners and drinks, for their theatrical magic, but most importantly for their unwavering belief in my work i am forever indebted to: Daniella Topol, Chay Yew, Lisa Portes, May Adrales, Ben Kamine, Mike Donahue, Marti Lyons, Elena Araoz and Mary Birnbaum.
- any playwright will tell you that they dream of an artistic home. for their generosity and support of the development of my work i'd like to thank: Jim Nicola, Linda Chapman, Ruben Polendo and the staff of the New York Theatre Workshop. Katherine Kovner, Alyssa Anderson, Jason Fitzgerald, and the incredible folks at the Playwrights Realm. Lou Moreno, Eduardo Machado and everyone at INTAR. John Dias, Stephanie Coen, and Jerry Ruiz for inviting me to Two River Theater. Bob Falls, Tanya Palmer, Neena Arndt, Henry Godinez, Andrew Knight and the remarkable staff at the Goodman Theater. Liz Carlson and Naked Angels.
- A special thanks is due to Jim Simpson, for committing to a production of my play a week after hearing a reading of it. The support and encouragement he gave me throughout the entire process is almost unheard of. Very few artistic directors will come into a room, and not only watch rehearsal, but get down and dirty with the actors, experimenting with choreography and checking in with the playwright to make sure their vision was being supported. I am grateful to Jim, Carol Ostrow, the incredible staff of the Flea Theater, and their courageous band of BATS for their magical production.
- My deepest and most heartfelt thanks to the visionary John Clinton Eisner and the extraordinary staff of the Lark Play Development Center. They have literally and figuratively given me the keys to the castle. They are an unbelievable support system and the community they have built there is the very lifeblood of the future of the American Theater. Special thanks to my friends (incredible artists in their own right who I learn from everyday) Lisa Rothe, Lloyd Suh, Andrea Hiebler, Michael Robertson, Suzy Fay, Jennifer Dorr White, TJ Weaver, Anna Kull and Tim O'Donnell.
- Along with the actors listed in the following plays, I am also in awe of the unbelievably talented, kind, ridiculously attractive, intelligent, actors who have found themselves reading my plays, some in public, some in my living room, some scraps and some fully formed pages, sharing their thoughts, talents, gifts and friendship: Kristen Connolly, Shannon Esper, Hannah Cabell, Bill Heck, Desmin Borges, JD Taylor, Josh Salt, Bill Army, Mikaela Feely-Lehmann, Patrick Heusinger, Steve Stout, Michael Micalizzi, Condola Rashad, Matthew Rauch, Michael Izquierdo, Molly Ward, Quinn VanAntwerp, Lucas Near-Verbrugghe, Hunter Canning, Birgit Huppuch, Jenny Ikeda, Michael Cumpsty, Armando Riesco, JJ Perez, Shirley Rumierek, Mike Crane, Sofia Gomez, Tim Heck, Peter Kim, Jon Norman Schneider, Rey Lucas Peña, Cory Michael Smith, Clea Alsip, Ruibo Qian, Julian Cihi, Andrew Hovelson, Carlo Alban, Bonnie Milligan,

Jonny Orsini, Kathryn Erbe, David Greenspan, Sue Jean Kim, Will Rogers, Sarah Sokolovic, Annie Purcell, Babak Tafti, Vanessa Wasche, Josh Barrett, Vayu O'Donnell, Annie Henk, Maggie Lacey, George West Carruth, Varin Ayala, Teddy Cañez, Gerry Rodriguez, Socorro Santiago, Cleo Gray, Leigh Dunham, Rodney To, Christina Lind, Gene Gallerano, Krysta Rodriguez, Monica Raymund, Frankie Alvarez, Scott Thomas, Christine Corpuz, Kristina Valada-Viars, Irene Sofia Lucio, Troy Deutsch, Hubert Point Du-Jour, John Russo, Mia Katigbaak, Jordan Mahome, Ching Valdes Aran, Vonia Arslanian, Matt Stadelmann, Alex Hanna, Kyle Brown, Samira Wiley, Randy Harrison, Alfredo Narcisco and anyone else I'm forgetting.

- If you're lucky, you meet one of the incredibly smart people in this business that also has a true love and passion for the art. And if you're very lucky, they become friends and advocates, and you are thankful everyday: Stephanie Ybarra, Geoffrey Jackson Scott, Jeremy Stoller, Morgan Jenness, Caridad Svich, Carrie Chapter, Leah Hamos, Beth Blickers, Sage Parker-Lang, Kate Navin, Christie Evangelisto, Sean Daniels, Jason Davids Scott, (uncle) Ralph Peña, Dan Safer and Micha Espinoza.
- Thank you to Sundance Institute, especially Philip Himberg and Ignacia Delgado, fierce advocates, beautiful people, for paying attention and for friendship.
- My incredible manager Henry Huang, a gentleman and a killer- thank you for the phone calls, friendship, and the support as needed... and the rest of Station 3.
- The incredible playwrights who inspire me everyday. I am grateful for your support, your friendship, and your work. I am so proud and honored to be part of your tribe: Daniel Sweren-Becker, Janine Nabers, Rey Pamatmat, Tanya Saracho, Bekah Brunstetter, matthew paul olmos, Victor Lesniewski, Krista Knight, Sharif Abu-Hamdeh, Jason Kim, Ben Kopit, Jon Caren, Josh Conkel, Rinne Groff, Alex Dinelaris, Carla Ching, Nick Jones, Leslye Headland, Alex Lubischer, Scott Barsotti, Elaine Romero, Andrea Thome, Mando Alvarado, Gaby Alter, Tommy Smith, Branden Jacobs-Jenkins, Stefanie Zadravec, Alice Austen, Ike Holter, Rob Askins, Rajiv Joseph, Dominique Morisseau, Greg Moss, Jess Brickman, Gabriel Jason Dean, Kimber Lee, Lynn Nottage, Rachel Bonds, Jose Rivera, David Henry Hwang, and Arthur Kopit.
- My amazing roommates Kim Director and Mike Carlsen, both brilliant actors and the best people to stay home and watch BRAVO with.
- Andrea Lauer, Anshuman Bhatia, Laura Brandel, Jon Cottle, Andrew Lazarow, for their brilliant design
- Melissa Lusk for her beautiful music (and matt roi berger for the first piece, and for being too busy for the second)— thank you for collaborating on plays, but also for creating an amazing soundscape to my life
- Many of my plays are about looking back, so I would be remiss if I didn't thank: Amelia Harris, David Terra, Derek Noone, Kit Ko, John Kincheloe, Hassan Elhaj, Danh Huynh, Maya Herr-Anderson, Quise Rodriguez, Rob

Medina, Diana (Ma) Hayes, Jenna (Daniels) Nohel, Tiffany Rose Brown, Dan Barlow, Elli Resvanis, Elizabeth Wueste, and Wilfred Torres.

finally, to my family, and especially my parents. They gave me a voice, but most importantly, they taught me how to use it. My parents immigrated here thirty years ago. I hope this collection is at least a fraction of what they've given me.

thank you all.

christopher oscar peña

Harlem, New York 11/2013

contributors

christopher oscar peña is an American playwright, originally from California, now residing in Manhattan. Selected plays include *maelstrom, icarus burns, alone above a raging sea, l(y)re, the suicide tapes* and *awe/struck*. His work has been developed or seen at the Public Theater, The Goodman Theater, Two River Theater, INTAR, the Ontological Hysteric Incubator, The Playwrights Realm, Son of Semele (LA), American Theater Company (Chicago), Rattlestick Playwrights Theater, the Old Vic, Theater For a New City, the Orchard Project, Naked Angels and the New York Theatre Workshop, among many others. After successful workshop productions in LA and New York, his play with composer Melissa Lusk *i wonder if it's possible to have a love affair that lasts forever? or things I found on craigslist* will close the University of Illinois-Chicago School of Theater's LAUNCH year season in 2014 . He is the creator and co-star of *80/20*, a new series for the web, which was recently named an Official Selection at the 2013 New Media Film Festival in LA, and won the 2013 Outstanding Achievement in writing from LAWEBFEST. His newest play *TINY PEOPLE (or, it gets better)* was a finalist for both the 2013 O'Neill Playwrights Conference and Sundance Theatre Lab, and was featured in the 2013 Crossing Borders Festival at Two Rivers Theater. Awards/fellowships: Latino Playwrights Award (Kennedy Center), New York Theatre Workshop Emerging Artist Fellow, Playwrights Realm Writing Fellow, Sewanee Writers Conference Fellow, US/UK Exchange (Old Vic New Voices). His play *a cautionary tail* received its professional world premiere at The Flea Theater in Tribeca in spring of 2013. He is working on a new commission from Chicago's Goodman Theater where he is in residence as a member of their Playwrights Unit. He was the Lark Play Development Centers 2012-2013 Van Lier Fellow and is currently a 2013-2014 Fellow in the Lark's Playwrights Workshop, where he is working on a new play. In 2014, he will be a fellow at the Sundance Institute Playwrights Retreat at Ucross and his first collection of published plays is forthcoming from NoPassport Press. He received his B.A. in Drama from UC Santa Barbara, where he studied with Naomi Iizuka, and holds an M.F.A. in Dramatic Writing from NYU's Tisch School of the Arts. He is represented by Henry Huang at Station 3.

Naomi Iizuka's plays include 36 VIEWS, POLAROID STORIES, LANGUAGE OF ANGELS, ANON(YMOUS), CONCERNING STRANGE DEVICES FROM THE DISTANT WEST, ALOHA, SAY THE PRETTY GIRLS, TATTOO GIRL, SKIN, GHOSTWRITTEN, AFTER A HUNDRED YEARS, STRIKE-SLIP, AT THE VANISHING POINT, HAMLET: BLOOD IN THE BRAIN (a collaboration with CalShakes and Campo Santo + Intersection for the Arts), and WAR OF THE WORLDS (written in collaboration with Anne Bogart and SITI Company.) Her plays have been produced by Berkeley Rep, the Goodman, the Guthrie, Cornerstone, Intiman, Children's Theater Company, the Kennedy Center, the Huntington Theater, Actors' Theatre of Louisville, GeVa, Laguna Playhouse, Portland Center Stage, the Public, Campo Santo + Intersection for the Arts, Dallas Theatre Center, the Brooklyn Academy of Music's "Next Wave Festival", Soho Rep, and the Edinburgh Festival. Her plays have been published by

12

Overlook Press, Playscripts, Smith and Kraus; Dramatic Publishing, Sun and Moon Press, and TCG. Iizuka is an alumna of New Dramatists and the recipient of a PEN/Laura Pels Award, an Alpert Award, a Joyce Foundation Award, a Whiting Writers' Award, a Stavis Award from the National Theatre Conference, a Rockefeller Foundation MAP grant, an NEA/TCG Artist-in-Residence grant, a McKnight Fellowship, a PEN Center USA West Award for Drama, Princeton University's Hodder Fellowship, and a Jerome Fellowship. She currently heads the MFA Playwriting program at the University of California, San Diego.

Stephanie Ybarra, an avid fan of her hometown San Antonio Spurs basketball team, still owns – and often wears – a pair of cowboy boots. With almost 15 years of experience under her belt (which matches her boots), Stephanie is currently putting her producing skills to work as Artistic Associate at The Public Theater. Previously, she spent three years up to one ear in scripts and the other ear in spreadsheets as Producing Director of The Playwrights Realm, where she produced early career playwrights like Anna Ziegler, Jen Silverman, and Gonzalo Rodriguez Risco. Stephanie made her New York producing debut in 2007 with the original production of Tarell McCraney's *The Brothers Size* at the Public Theater's Under the Radar Festival (directed by Tea Alagic), for which she received the inaugural Producer's Chair Award from the Foundry Theater. Since then she has produced for Cherry Lane Theater (Mentor Project), HERE Arts Center (*Finding Ways*, by Snehal Desai, directed by Erik Pearson), Women's Project (*We Play for the Gods*, by the 2010-2012 Lab), Ars Nova's A.N.T Fest (*One Night With Rael*, by Timothy Charles Brown, directed by Snehal Desai), Studio 42 (*Billy Witch* by Greg Moss, directed by Erik Pearson) and INTAR (The HPRL Writers Group). She also serves as Casting Director for Two River Theater Company's Crossing Borders Festival. Stephanie started in her native Texas, working in Marketing and Development for Dallas Theater Center and Dallas Children's Theater, and then spent time in Boston serving as Deputy Director of Operations for Citizen Schools, a Boston-based national after school program. Roles such as Associate Managing Director of New Play Production at Yale Repertory Theatre, Executive Producer of Summer Cabaret 2007 and Interim General Manager for Two River Theater Company round out her tri-state credits. Stephanie is a card-carrying member of the LXP Producing Collective, belongs t the Women's Project 2010-2012 Producer's Lab, and serves on the board of the Yale Latino Alumni Association. She holds a BFA from Baylor University, an MFA from Yale School of Drama, and a deep belief in the power of the post-it note.

Stephen Stout is an actor and producer and friend of cp's. As a theater administrator, he's worked for some cool buildings like The Flea Theater, The Old Vic in London, and The Public. As an actor, he's appeared in some cool things at some cool places. A bunch of those were written by cp.

Foreword

I met Chris when he was a first year student at UC-Santa Barbara. I was teaching a class in playwriting and Chris showed up one day. I don't think Chris was supposed to be in my class. If I'm remembering correctly, he wasn't on my roster of enrolled students. There was a wait list and I don't think he was on that either. I'm pretty sure I turned him away, but he came back. As anyone who knows Chris knows, he is very persistent. Chris kept coming back. And I'm so glad he did.

I think by the time Chris graduated, he had taken every playwriting class I taught at UCSB more than once. Chris was part of a remarkable community of writers that had somehow found their way to UCSB. They turned out to be some of the most eclectic, eccentric, passionate, and talented playwrights I've ever known. If you know UCSB, you know how improbable it is that this community of playwrights flourished here. UCSB is a school best known for beer pong and setting couches on fire. It's a school renowned for its Bacchanalian excess and good surfing. And yet somehow, from out of nowhere emerged this vibrant community of playwrights. They were kids from Anaheim and Pacoima, San Jose and Oakland, kids who had never seen a play, and here they were all of a sudden writing their own plays. And they were really, really good. They were also unlike anything else I had ever seen or heard before or since. It was an extraordinary group of writers, and Chris was one of the best and brightest among them.

From day one, it felt like Chris was writing these tantalizing messages in a bottle. He was chronicling his world and the people in it. Chris has always had a keen ear for the vernacular of his generation. He had an intuition about the stories of his particular historical moment. He was attuned to the ways in which social media was transforming how we communicate with others, how we create an identity, how we make sense of the narrative of our lives. He was also wrestling with the shifting cultural landscape of race, ethnicity, and sexual orientation of his moment in time. There was always a palpable ambition to take part in larger, cultural conversations in Chris' work, and a voracious inquisitiveness that fueled the writing. There was an impulse to bring forth all that scary, funny, sad, messy, weird, profound, wondrous stuff that makes up human experience. It was there back when he first started writing, and it's still there now.

Chris always wrote a lot. He rewrote even more. He put his plays up along with his classmates in a small black box theatre. Chris also read every play he could get his hands on. He traveled great distances to see plays. He lived to talk about theatre and playwriting every chance he could get. I brought a lot of guest artists to campus when I was at UCSB, artists like Luis Alfaro, Chay Yew, Les Waters, Campo Santo, Jonathan Moscone, Lisa Portes, Carlos Murillo, David Adjmi, Cynthia Hopkins, Daniel Alexander Jones, and many, many others. Chris was in the front row of every master class, every workshop, every performance. He was soaking it all in.

Among that amazing group of writers that Chris came of age with at UCSB, a handful are still writing plays. Some pursued other professions. One young woman went to teach English in Spanish Harlem. Another is raising two beautiful daughters in Orange County. Some fell down the rabbit hole of addiction and alcoholism. I hear that one of the writers went to work for a production company that films pornographic videos somewhere in the San Fernando Valley. And then there's Chris. Chris is very talented. He has a voice and he has something to say. He also works very hard and has an enthusiasm that is unsurpassed. But what struck me, what has always struck me most about Chris was his hunger. Chris was hungry to make theatre, and that hunger has propelled him forward against all odds to write his plays, to find his tribe, and make a life for himself in theatre. There's a lot of hunger in Chris and also a lot of joy. I know few other artists who love the sheer act of making theatre as much as Chris. I am excited by the plays he has written, and I look forward with great anticipation to the plays that he will write.

Naomi Iizuka
Playwright, Head of MFA Playwriting, UCSD

Introduction

As I'm sitting down to write this, I've decided to attempt to position myself in the very spot in which all of chris peña's plays are located. I've got MSNBC on (mute), watching images of the world today flashing across the screen. I'm listening to my online radio station playing only Billboard's Top 100. And, I'm flipping between Twitter, Facebook, Instagram, and this word document every 60-90 seconds. All of this is to say that I am sitting smack dab in the middle of "Now."

The themes and ideas of chris's plays often come right out of a national conversation, or a collective generational psyche – often, it's both. In the case of *a cautionary tail*, chris took on the timely topic of "Tiger Moms" during a moment in which the media was saturated with a debate over the merits of strict parenting techniques. *...things i found on craigslist* taps in to the deeply universal experience of an existential crisis (by way of a high school reunion), and reflects back to us the best and worst of what it means to be an adult. *icarus burns** is a personal favorite of mine because the expansive socio political themes of internal racism, classicism and immigration come in the context of deeply personal struggles with familial loyalty and domestic abuse (the imaginary talking bird also scores major points with me). All of these plays represent a sort of cultural snap shot of America today – they capture a specific kind of Now, which has come to be a hallmark of chris peña's writing.

The thing that makes chris's plays unique, however, is the extra step he takes to tell the story of Now. chris plays fast and loose with form and structure and manages to not only tell the content of the stories of today, but to also tell those stories in the same way we receive them in the so-called real world. Let me put it to you another way: you will never find a unit set in a play by christopher oscar peña. The episodic, fragmented, sometimes nonlinear way his stories unfold are part of the contemporary-ness of his work. His scenes – disjointed though they may seem at first glance – riff off one another and sometimes employ vastly different (albeit complementary) techniques to accomplish their goal. Even the worlds within these plays contain multiple realities, each with its own set of rules and a distinct purpose. The end result is a kind of theatrical prism, refracting and reflecting our evolving humanity.

This is the part where I start to really geek out because each of these plays has, in my opinion, the most important virtue of all. And that is theatricality. It sounds a little like a "duh" moment, but the more plays I read the more I feel like I'm reading scripts made for a screen instead of a stage. Each of the plays in this anthology embraces its theatrical medium. Whether it's the ever-dramatic Tiger Mom in *a cautionary tail*, or Lorenzo in *icarus burns*, there is always some element that pays homage to live theater and an audience's imagination. It is this invitation to theatergoers to suspend disbelief and come along for the ride that allows for the sweeping landscape that is often the backdrop for chris's stories. I cannot overstate the value of the importance of this inherent collaboration with the audience in chris peña's work - though he is part of a generation of writers raised on television and film, his plays require a certain imaginative presence from all those who encounter them.

I could go on forever about these plays, and the others chris is currently working on (don't even get me started on the brilliance of TINY PEOPLE, his riff on Chekhov's Three Sisters). But, given that I am constantly giving chris a hard time about the length of his plays, I will end my note here and let you get on with the adventure that is exploring a play written by christopher oscar peña. After you've read them, go ahead and produce one. You'll have a fantastic time living in a peña world, steeped in his signature mix of pop culture and politics. #ipromise

Stephanie Ybarra
Artistic Associate, Public Theater, New York

icarus burns is a work-in-progress, not included in this collection

millenials, the internet and just what the hell do you think you're going to do with the rest of your life: christopher oscar peña – a user's guide*

*written by stephen stout somewhat earnestly in the style of christopher oscar peña

greetings
fair reader
book purchaser
browser at drama bookshop
greetings

you are about to spend some time in the world of christopher oscar peña

from here on out we'll call him cp

cause you're family now
a member of the posse
the a-list (as the man himself would ironically posit)
you're in cp-land
most likely for the first time

i feel
as someone who has lived in cp's world for the better part of a decade
a decade of seeing the sun come up after planning world domination
of parties and weddings and concerts and play openings
impossible to get tickets that always manage to appear because cp wills them to
(full disclosure: i'm not always at the concerts)
that you might need a little guide
a primer
some pro-tips
that'll help you find your way
so imagine this introduction
as the little paperclip with eyeballs that used to be in microsoft word
you know
(i'm not that old am i?!)
the little anthropomorphic beast you'd click on in high school computer lab
to avoid doing actual work
since it's more fun to ask a cartoon paperclip the great questions
than wrangle with a blank page
anyways i'm a little off track
like you might be
later

so
i say to you
if you're lost

if you're confused
check back here
and you'll find what you need
to get you to the other side
the back cover
covered with more quotes that'll help you grapple with this extraordinary man
and his extraordinary plays

so
let's move forward shall we?
since we can
and the majority of the people, animals and greater powers
you're about to encounter
find it impossible

the stage directions

always read these out loud
they're generally hilarious
they're not really an omniscient narrator
they're really cp
offering suggestions
for what might happen at the beginnings and the endings of things

when you're in production
it's your job to unpack these
and choose what you could do
and be fun and entertaining and colorful
to portray the sense or feel of the stage directions
even when they're impossible to literally do
like "the sound of facebook exploding"
what the hell are you supposed to do with that?
well
make facebook explode in a theatrically clever way
maybe it's a dance
maybe you have a mad genius sound designer
maybe it's absolute silence
maybe the actor looks at the audience for the first time
make a choice

(it always comes back to choices)

capitalization

what is this foreign concept called capitalization?

the content

this world
this world you are about to enter
to explore
to enjoy
to be challenged and frightened and amused by
has some rules

these rules
they change

from play to play
moment to moment

sometimes inevitably
most times without warning

roll with them
some are meant to be understood and deciphered in that good symbolist way
others are meant to change the trajectory of the story
of how it's being told
and how you
the audience
is meant to experience it
roll with these
hop on board like it's your first roller coaster and hold on for dear life

some examples are probably helpful
so
an e-vite to your high school reunion can suddenly make you realize
that ten years have gone by
and you and those you love
are far
very far
from where they thought they'd be
and yet there are angels
or devils
let's call them forces
that are fighting over your soul
and causing you to remain stagnate
trapped in yourself
but you don't know that
cause who sees angels or devils anymore?
or
a token from your childhood
a silly moment of abandon

can
(thanks to the handy dandy and constantly present internet)
become the defining traumatic moment of your life
(cause that's how things can work these days)
and your mother
(who is, of course, a tiger)
might suddenly appear and trap you in a jungle
a metaphorical jungle
or maybe, more boldly, an actual jungle
a totally real, frightening labyrinth
where the only way you can get out
is by pushing yourself to make the choice you've been avoiding your whole life
stuff like that
y'know the easy stuff

there will also be jokes
many lols
our modern urban patois thoroughly captured
and skewered
in all it's self-important, overly abbreviated, profane and half-cocked glory

there will also be references
joy division and facebook and andy warhol references
as cp says "the things that makes us who we are"
tokens of the things
the pop cultural things
objects
holy relics
the detritus that fills up our lives today
these tokens
these emblems of who you are
these will be useful as well
and possess life-changing meaning
or they might be just be cool to remember
you may never know

so what i'm saying
what i'm saying
is you're gonna need to do some of the work

the characters

they're all good guys
they are trying their best
they often don't say what they mean
they often are haunted by something
usually someone

they believe in concepts like "the one"
or "the right choice"
or "destroying someone completely because they hurt you"
they're a little bit of a mess

they're mostly young
they thought everything was going to be perfect
that they should check off the items on the grocery list their parents handed them
the one entitled "how to be happy, moneyed and win for your entire life"
and then things work out
most of them are unprepared for life's chaos

most are running from something
and that something will probably catch up with them in a few scenes
they all mean well
read their actions as if they're doing what they believe is best in this moment

they're probably really well dressed and have cool tattoos
if today wasn't the worst day of their entire lives
you'd probably really love to hang out with them
they're extensions of cp's own heart
loyalty
truth
friends like family
wanting to be better
reinventing yourself
finding the six to ten people you can go through the tough shit with
and constantly find yourself awake at 4 or 5 in the morning
thinking "how did i get here again"
and then remembering
and then laughing your ass off
that's what's important to these people

oh
and if they're magic
they'll probably cut you with a knife fashioned from the leg bone of your first love
don't fuck with the magic ones

oh wait this one's important
when they talk
if they seem to get a bit highfalutin
to overreach in their language
to say grand things like "these days i don't know what to believe anymore"
imagine they are saying it in a manner that is awkward and fumbled
it's normal people trying to make their words reflect the height of their feelings
like when you're thinking of non-cliché things to write in a love letter
or when you sext someone you probably shouldn't

at an embarrassing hour of the night
or when you're writing an apology email to a friend who you haven't seen in ages
because you did something bad
real bad
they sometimes talk like we all do in those moments
those moments
when we need to talk fancy
to get what we want

oh
and
to repeat
all of them should look really, really cool

repetition

you'll notice that things repeat
words repeat
structures repeat
in the text

these moments are meant to build
to emphasize those moments in life when we need to muster our powers
to taste our choices
to roll them around in our mouths
like when we pretend to savor a fine wine to affect being cultured
or not

maybe the character is nervous and just needs to delay moving forward
to stay in this moment
this one moment
until they can make a stab at what to do in the next
or it just sounds really cool
you should read these out loud
that's when they tend to make their meaning known

which reminds me

line endings

if you're saying the lines
don't pause between the line endings
the line endings are units of thought
one action
one moment of meaning
then you move to the next one
even when the next one

is a complete contradiction of where you just were

make it natural and off the cuff
even when your heart is breaking
or when you're talking to your nemesis who is now mysteriously a vulture
like an actual vulture
with the wings and the beak
even in the weird times
especially in the weird times
natural
off the cuff
and fast

tempo

these plays are supposed to move like a bat out of hell
don't stop
don't stop
don't stop

move forward
make a choice and then make another choice

move forward
don't just feel something do something

move forward
the characters can't so you fucking better

go fast

that is all

tone

it's sad when it's sad
then it shifts

it's funny when it's funny
then it shifts

embrace the shifts
don't fix them
don't explain them
fully embrace them

music

ok two kinds of song here
the first kind you listen to on your ipod
or in cp's most ideal of ideal worlds: your warn-in record player
given to you by a hot dude
there's always an impossible to get hot dude
cp probably has some true-life examples of these dudes
if you see him ask him about these dudes
i officially give you permission
wait where was i?
oh right music like the kind you listen to on your ipod or phone or music doohickey
ask your cool friend
the one who is in a band or has tattoos or spends far too much time on pitchfork
ask your cool friend what they listen to
have them make a list of what bands and tracks aren't totally known
but are totally about to be bat shit famous
boom
there's your soundtrack, pre-show and intermission mixes

now to the second kind of song
the latter kind of song
these should sound like the former
these are the kind you sing
like you
not at karaoke
like you just burst into song
sorta like a musical
but no kick lines
if you do a kick line
cp will cry
these are sung to move the show forward

directors
use these moments to propel the show and it's themes forward
they are to be sung with full commitment by imperfect voices

ok so a little like karaoke

make them pop-y and fun
(though in regards to ...*things i found on craiglist*, i defy you to write catchier tunes than melissa lusk. google her and her band boy girl party for an amuse bouche)

like the stage directions
these are moments of theatrical possibility

26

to be clever and cool
make a choice
(again with the choices)
(and the repetition)
(the repetition)
(the repetition)

final thoughts

everyone thinks there are plays about millenials
really they're thinking of gen-x plays
or in-yer-face plays
or angry young man plays
or basically any play that has a twenty-to-thirty something in it
there have been millenials in plays
they're the ones texting when they should be listening
they're the ones who pontificate and can't pay for anything
they're the ones who live at home either in the suburbs or the upper east side
they're meant to be mocked
they've had plays written about them right?
well fuck no they haven't
cp is one of the first millennial playwrights to actually portray and atomize
millennials
as more than a cheap joke for boomer subscribers
i think that's kinda important
anyways
enjoy these plays
they're really special to me
(i was eduardo in ...*things i found on craigslist* and kaelen in *a cautionary tail*)
cp is one of my oldest and best friends
these plays are messy, epic, hilarious, bitchy
filled with tears and tigers and angels
like a night out with cp
enjoy
and remember to drink water

--Stephen Stout
Brooklyn, 2013

*Stephen Stout is an actor and producer and friend of cp's. As a theater
administrator, he's worked for some cool buildings like The Flea Theater, The
Old Vic in London, and The Public. As an actor, he's appeared in some cool
things at some cool places. A bunch of those were written by cp.*

a cautionary tail

by christopher oscar peña

TO

      Janine Nabers
      Rey Pamatmat
      Bekah Brunstetter
      Branden Jacobs-Jenkins
      Tanya Saracho
      Victor Lesniewski
      Krista Knight
      matthew paul olmos
      Josh Conkel
      Jon Caren
      Rob Askins

for giving me shoulders to stand on

and **FOR**

      Steve Stout
              just because

a cautionary tail had its world premiere production at The Flea Theater, New York (Jim Simpson, Artistic Director and Carol Ostrow, Producing Director). The play opened on June 10, 2013 under the direction of Benjamin Kamine. The design team included David Meyer (Set), Andrea Lauer (Costume), Jonathan Cottle (Lights), Jeremy S. Bloom (Sound) and Laura Brandel (Movement Director). The stage manager was Anne Huston.

The cast was as follows: Bobby Foley *(tiger/tin)*, Cleo Gray *(vivienne)*, Tony Vo *(luke)*, Barron Bass *(derek)*, Stephen Stout *(kaelan)*, Madeleine Bundy *(brandi)*, Bonnie Milligan *(koren)*, Marlowe Holden *(joanna)*, Jacquelyn Revere *(sonya)*, Alex Grubbs *(traveling salesman/ jack/ william)*. Alton Alburo, Matt Bovee, Jenelle Chu, Sasha Diamond, Aaron Parker Fouhey, Karen Eilbacher, Alex J. Gould, Christiine Lee, and Evan Maltby *(ensemble)*. The following actors joined the ensemble at extension: Krystina Bailey, Orlando Rivera, Kate Thulin, and Ramon Olmos Torres.

---

a cautionary tail was commissioned by New York University's Graduate Acting Program (Mark Wing-Davey, Chair). The play received a workshop production in the Atlas Theater from December 1 – 5, 2012 under the direction of Kyle Fabel. The design team included Rebecca Philips (set), Kathleen Doyle (costume), Anshuman Bhatia (lights), Fitz Patton (sound) and Whitney Hunter (choreography).

The cast was as follows: David Lam *(tiger/tin)*, Ruibo Qian *(vivienne)*, Julian Cihi *(luke)*, Robbie Willliams *(derek)*, Ross Cowan *(kaelan)*, Anne Troup *(brandi/ joanna)*, Marinda Anderson *(koren/ sonya)*, Andrew Hovelson *(traveling salesman/ jack/ william)*, Dina Shihabi *(dancer/ensemble)*.

well, now i'm back at home and
i'm looking forward to this life i live
you know it's gonna haunt me
so hesitation to this life i give

-   *spaceman*
        The Killers

---

i've seen the troubles and the evils,
of this world
i've seen the ones who can succeed,
but always lose,
i've seen what's left,
of poor technology and work,
and watched them dying as they,
leave their ship of fools.

and they left it for you-
all of this is for you.

-   *the drawback*
        Joy Division

characters:

luke wood-   *seventeen. impulsive. a very american, chinese boy.*

vivienne wood-   *eighteen. calm. thoughtful. strong willed. trying to make it work.*

the tiger-   *an androgynous leader. the mother(fucker) who rules this jungle.*

also plays   **tin wong**   *an asian man who has lost his way.*

derek-   *vivienne's boyfriend. eighteen. a black man who is japanese.*

brandi-   *a rich, bitchy, white girl. thinks she's so cool. lukes BFF forever.*

also plays   **joanna davidowitz**   *thirties. corporate power chick.*

koren-   *another one of lukes BFF's. wiser than brandi. loves to sing. lesbian?*

also plays   **sonya washington**   *thirties. wears the pants. power woman at the office.*

kaelan burke-   *super hot. hipster musician type. grounded. open and exploring.*

the old fashioned traveling salesman-   *just that. and magical. loves his job. secretly nice.*

also plays   **william grant**   *coporate guy. snarky. enjoys his job, which is like fucked up.*

also plays   **jack**   *an unkempt, but charming man. the guy who means it.*

setting:

new york city
      the wood family apartment-
            the living room
            viviennes room
            lukes room
     a record store: OTHER MUSIC
     a park in chinatown
     a corporate office
     across the street from a kids private school (say st. annes)
     an office in china

the jungle: the tigers den

time:

a few years ago and a few years from now

     and a place right in the middle that stretches on forever

notes:

-it is important that the jungle world feel different from the rest of the play

-this play works best when it moves quickly, expertly, fluidly and things bleed
into each other

-this play is about opposites. east meets west. tradition versus progress. speed
and stagnancy. old and new. the past and the future. holding on and forgetting.
the more you play with theatricalizing these themes, the better.

-the gestures are meant to act as a physical representation of forward movement,
progression that is too fast, a ground that we cant stand on, because we are
searching for balance. its meant to contrast the normal paced-ness of everything
else that is happening. sometimes we, our minds, the world, are moving faster
than we think – let the actors experience this and make it real in the moments
where it is listed.

-this play loves sound and light and dark and shadows and fragments and
missing pieces.

-i imagine the dance breaks being hipster/ambience rock: girls, my gold mask,
deerhunter, twin shadow, neon indian, washed out, the 1975, muse, etc etc.

-finally, the first act of this play should feel like a neon pop music video. it should feel like the movie spring breakers. and the second act, should feel like kids, all the color drained away. think of it as an homage.

act one.

scene.

> *darkness*
> *the kind of darkness you might find in a cave*
> *sounds of dripping*
> *water*
> *sounds of*
> *whipping*
> *air*
> *sounds of deep breathing in a cave*
> *almost as if the cave is alive*
> *and then light punctuates the air*
> *fighting its way in*
> *the entire cast*
> *save the tiger*
> *comes out*

1
a myth

2
a story

3
a truth

4
a place to begin

5
where to begin

6
at the very beginning

7
too late for that

8
somewhere in the middle

9
somewhere where the past has already affected the present

10
a place with baggage

11
heavy baggage

12
history

13
a myth

14
a story

15
a truth

16
a true story

17
a made up story

18
a place from which to move forward

19
a place not to go

20
before its too late

21
its already too late

22
or is it

23
a tiger

all
a tiger

the tiger reveals itself
first in darkness

a silhouette
    and then it emerges
regal and proud
    the tiger is fabulous and fabulously dressed
high fashion couture
    she is an androgynous beast of beauty
she speaks to those who it commands
      she is posed and in control
    of
      every
    syllable

the tiger
you must regard tradition
tradition is history
tradition is order
you must respect the natural order of the universe
of mother and father
ancient rules cast on stone never to be forgotten
keep tradition and the world keeps spinning
break with tradition and suffer the consequences
of all those who have come before
my will is your law
because i know better than you
only when you have lived
only when you have experienced
only when you have followed the paths marked out for you
only then will you understand
only then will you be wise
until then you are just a fool
and that is what i am here for
to lead you until you are not

    with a wave of her hand, the ensemble vanishes
    and then the tiger
      breaks
        the tiger breaks and her
    well her
      her real ATTITUDE is exposed
  she is a
    DIVA

the tiger
so here is the thing
its simple really
just do as i say
you may not understand now
but you will someday
and then you will love me

and kiss me
and thank me
and say
tiger tiger
you were right
you were right the whole time
and i will not say i told you so
because i
i am not that kind of tiger
instead i will hug you and lick your face and say
well
i told you so
im only doing it because i love you
love
what a strange word
so do as i say
and don't question me
don't push my boundaries
because if you do
i might eat you up
get in my way and i will crush you
im only doing whats best for you

        and then with a flick of her wrist
    the ensemble emerges from the shadows
       and then a dance
   a ritualistic calling out
     the dance
       the ritual
    the movement is not realistic
      it is stylized
      and harsh
      and precise
       it is made up of gestures
    some gestures are done by everyone at the same time
   others are broken up
  and done by only a few
      it is chaotic
    and frenetic
      and schizophrenic
    some of the gestures are
      a tai chi exercise
     a chinese dance
      the playing of a violin
        over and over
       and over and over and over
      and over and over

another tai chi exercise
banging your head against a wall
rocking out to an eighties british rock song
playing the piano
dancing like your madonna in front of an audience
a gesture that symbolizes a starvation for affection
starvation for love   .
a hug
another tai chi exercise
another chinese dance
east meets west
running fast with no energy at the end
the snapping of a photograph
writing kanji in the sky
as then the ritual is over
and everything vanishes.

scene.

> new york city
> a park in chinatown
> a park bench
> maybe a chain link fence surrounding a basketball court
> its early in the evening

> derek sits on a park bench looking around
> he is seventeen
> a strong framed black man
> he seems quiet
> introspective
> he is hard to read
> he is looking for something
> or someone
> checks his watch
> do people still wear those?
> he checkes his iphone

> in another part of the park
> there is a STATUE OF A

MAN

> the statue is dressed in a suit
> the type an old traveling

salesman might wear

> the statue is PURPLE from head

to toe

> in its hand it hold his hat... upside down
> his briefcase is on the floor in front of him...

open

> sounds of the city
> a honk here
> a car there
> we hear a song that seems old
> from another time
> another place
> because it is
> an old chinese song
> muffled words
> it is haunting
> and then

> vivienne arrives
> shes also seventeen

rushed
shes very pretty with sad eyes

vivienne
sorry

derek
i was starting to think you weren't going to show up

vivienne
i told you i was on my way

derek
thirty minutes ago

vivienne
it took me twenty minutes to convince my brother to keep his mouth shut and cover for me

derek
whys your brother such a little dick

vivienne
i don't know
hes just immature

derek
how much time do we have

vivienne
an hour
shes taking the 715 train back from connecticut

derek
i wonder if your mom will ever stop being so overbearing

vivienne
she just wants us to do well
that's all
im supposed to be practicing the violin right now

derek
do you even like playing that thing

vivienne
i don't know

a moment

vivienne
id rather be taking pictures
but she doesn't think photography is a viable career

derek
why do you do it

vivienne
to appease her

derek
i meant take pictures

vivienne
see that spot

she points at a spot in the distance

vivienne
when i was younger
there was this guy that would come out and have his lunch here every day at the
same time
he would sit here and watch everyone
take in the sun
take in the noise
and he would talk to anyone who would listen
i was always fascinated by his stories
he was this hippie thai guy
big hair
had a son in stockholm
worked as a masseur in a little storefront around the corner that's now a deli
one day he told me
today i say goodbye to you
he was leaving for australia that night to see about a girl
that's what he said
to see about a girl
never saw him again after that
and now sometimes
i start to forget what he looks like

*she pulls the camera up to her face and snaps a
picture*

vivienne
one day itll be too late you know

a moment

vivienne
are you scared

derek
of what
no

vivienne
everyone is scared of something

derek
what is there to be afraid of

vivienne
change
big decisions
wrong decisions
these moments

derek
we're not the first high schoolers to have to pick which college to go to

vivienne
i got into harvard

derek
so that's it then

vivienne
i didn't say that

derek
what else is there
im going to school in california
loyola is the only place that gave me money
im not like you
i didn't get full rides to westmont
and nyu
and ucla
and penn
i have to take it

vivienne
that's not my fault

derek
whats that supposed to mean

vivienne
nothing

derek
no say it

vivienne
i didn't mean anything by it

derek
i want to hear you say it vivienne

vivienne
i told you to work harder

derek
so now im not smart enough for you right
now im not good enough

vivienne
that's not what i said
being smart and working hard are two different things

derek
so im lazy

vivienne
im not saying youre anything
stop putting words in my mouth

derek
that's what it sounds like

vivienne
i just
i wish this was easier

derek
well it isn't

vivienne
i know

silence
a moment
like that moment on a windshield

where the crack appears
and youre watching it ripple out
right
before it
shatters

vivienne
what if i came to california too
theres this school
calarts

derek
what about it

vivienne
i got in
as a photography major

derek
your mom would never let you

vivienne
its not her choice

derek
are you kidding
you have to sneak out of the house to see me
almost a full
grown up adult
and she dictates every single little thing you do
she would never let you go

vivienne
its my choice

derek
shes not going to pay for it
youll never be able to afford it

vivienne
i have a full scholarship
i can do it without her

derek
youre going to defy your mother
YOU
vivienne woods
your father is one thing

he might let you go
but your mother
youd break before your mouth found the words

vivienne
i love you

> *silence*
> > *silence*
> > > *silence*
> > > *pieces of the old chinese song fill the space*

vivienne
will you say something

derek
thank you

vivienne
i don't
i wont
i don't think you should say it back if you don't mean it
but
but
but
ive been saying it to you
and every time you say thank you
it just
like you know
hurts or something
and im trying to like
i don't know
figure out my life or whatever
and im trying to make these really hard choices
and i don't want to come to california just for you
but i mean if you don't love me then i should just know
because these choices will affect
like the rest of my life

> *he grabs her and kisses her*

derek
do you remember
when we first met
i said
i said
IM japanese

vivienne
yea

derek
i looked at you and said
i know you see a black man
and you think american
or african american
but i was raised in japan
my whole life
so even though you look at me and see this one thing
and categorize it in your mind in this box that you understand
in this box that you are used to
it doesn't actually fit there
think of me as japanese
culturally
mentally
emotionally
think of me as japanese
that is my language
i am japanese

he says a japanese phrase

vivienne
what does that mean

derek
ive never said i love you to anyone
in japanese there is no real equivalent anymore
it seems like something old fashioned that people from the past would say to each
other
its not something i am used to

she kisses him

vivienne
will you say it
just so i know
so i understand
my way

derek
i love you

vivienne
i love you too

a moment

derek
that's a beautiful song

vivienne
they've been here since before i existed
it's a very old song

they listen for a moment

vivienne
i want to go to california

derek
but your mother will never let you

vivienne
ive already turned down harvard

> *they hold hands and listen to the music*
> *after a moment*
> *they get up and go*
> *as they go*
> *vivienne stops in front of the statue and looks*
at it

> *she drops some change into its hat and walks away*
> *after a moment*
> *the statue COMES TO LIFE*
> *he moves*
> *he looks around*
> *and then...*
> *he follows them*

scene.

a record store
we'll say its OTHER MUSIC on 4th st and lafayette
hipsters
musicians
the kind of people that listen to music on vinyl are hanging out looking at
records

luke is trying to fit in perusing around the store
he is young, gay, and asian
good looking
cool
but not as cool as he wants to be
he picks up a record and flips it over

after a moment
kaelan comes up to him
kaelan is actually cool
or
hes probably "as cool" as luke is
but hes not trying to be more than he is
hes comfortable in his skin
scruffy, white t, skinny jeans, boots, you get the deal

kaelan
that's a really good record
definitely one of my favorites

luke
ive never heard it

kaelan
love will tear us apart

luke
which one is that

kaelan
oh come on man

kaelan sings the song
kaelan
when routine bites hard
and ambitions are low
and resentment rides high
but emotions wont grow

but luke isn't getting it
kaelan is trying really hard, but like cool you know
its totally cute

kaelan
and we're changing our way
taking different roads
NO?

luke
um

kaelan
love
love will tear us apart again

is luke embarrassed a little?
are people watching?

luke
oh yea!

but he doesn't really get it

kaelan
love
love will tear us apart again

luke
i saw the movie

kaelan
control

luke
yea
so i thought i should get it
and like listen to them

kaelan
that record changed my life

luke
cool
ill definitely listen to it

kaelan
do you come in here a lot

luke
no
this is my first time
im meeting my friends for tai chi around the corner but im
im early

kaelan
you to tai chi
that's awesome

luke
wait
are you
youre kaelan burke

kaelan
yea

luke
luke wood
                    kaelan doesn't know who that is
luke
you graduated two years ago from stuy

kaelan
yea

luke
i was a freshman

kaelan
oh rad

luke
i thought you like went to stanford or something

kaelan
i did
for a while
but it wasn't
it wasn't for me you know

luke
you dropped out of stanford

kaelan
yea

luke
why
who does that

kaelan
i do
it just didn't make sense to spend all that money on something i wasn't totally
happy with

luke
what did your parents say

kaelan
they were whatever about it
less money for them to spend

luke
crazy

kaelan
no big deal

luke
are you still dating that chick
lisa or whatever

kaelan
nah
we broke up a while ago
didn't really fit
what about you
are you seeing anyone

luke
i don't really like any of the guys at my school

kaelan
oh right on
im sort of between things right now
trying to figure out what fits

luke
oh
oh
yea
that's cool

kaelan
we're too young to be settling down and making like permanent choices you know

luke
sure
so what
like what are you up to
since youre not in school

kaelan
this

luke
what

kaelan
i work here

luke
at the record store

kaelan
yep

luke
whoa

kaelan
what

luke
you work in a record store
like in a john hughes movie

kaelan
yea well
someone has to i guess

luke
right
i just
i guess i never though about it
who actually works in a record store

kaelan
i do

luke
right
yea
that's awesome

kaelan
i love music

luke
are you in a band
tell me youre in a band

kaelan
guilty

luke
guitar

kaelan
drums

luke
youre like so relaxed though

kaelan
probably cuz i take it out on the drums

luke
definitely

kaelan
i think that customer needs something
he like keeps eyeing me
i cant tell if he actually needs help or if hes just eye fucking me

luke
probably both
i'd- i'd fuck you-
i'd- i'd eye fuck you

kaelan
you just said that

luke
yep
so i got to get to tai chi

kaelan
you want that record

luke
do you have it on cd

kaelan
don't get that shit on cd man
its joy division

luke
i don't have a record player

kaelan
but you were looking at the vinyl section

luke
right
well
i don't have a record player
but
i want to be the kind of guy who does

kaelan
you just said that too

luke
yea well
my sister says im impulsive
its yea
i should go

kaelan
what are you doing later

luke
homework

kaelan
ha
that's cute

luke
you work in a record store
that's cute
did this throw kaelan off his game or did he find it cute?

luke
im gonna meet my friends in columbus park in chinatown
it's a couple blocks from my house
so we study there

kaelan
oh yea
that's rad
i play basketball there sometimes

luke
cool
maybe ill see you there

                              luke is about to go but then ...
kaelan
listen
                              kaelan points up

luke
what

kaelan
no-
just listen

                         and then
          the world is filled with the sound of joy divisions "love will tear us apart"
                    it EXPLODES into a technicolor dream

                         and suddenly
                    they are in the pop music video
                              of
                         their lives

scene.

joanna davidowitz sits in her office
floor to ceiling windows
certificates and plaques on the walls
this office is in a building run by a huge corporation
we're talking global engineering
you can see the best view of manhattan from this office

shes on the phone

joanna
send them all to china
ive been saying it for years
we need our strongest out there
its time
forgive me if its un-AMERICAN to say that
but seeing as how we're a capitalist society
and this
this is a capitalist company
it seems almost un-AMERICAN to do the opposite

there is a knock at the door
she keeps talking

joanna
exactly
im with you bob

another knock

joanna
come in
ned
oh hes fine
but hes not our man
josh is our man
yes
he has his priorities in the right place

tin wong opens the door and approaches
very mildly
maybe head bowed
hes terrified of interrupting
he is well dressed-
but not too well dressed
and well mannered
he blends in
joanna motions for him to sit down
he does so

joanna
right right

he has no family
moving him will be easy and efficient
my two favorite things
perfect
perfect
ill make the call right now
whats that bob
exactly
talk soon
ciao
tin
what can i do for you

tin
i know youre busy

a moment

joanna
so get to it

tin
i wanted to talk to you about brett phillips

joanna
what about him

tin
the promotion

joanna
hes going to be out celebrating all night

tin
i know you have your reasons for making choices the way you do

joanna
that's right
nothings an accident here

tin
and i don't want to overstep my boundaries

joanna
then don't

tin
i would never want to do that
i love my job

i am happy here
this is the best place to be an engineer

joanna
we think so too
so im glad to hear you feel that way too tin

tin
but i am here because

joanna
because

tin
because i have been with this company for five years

joanna
and they've been a great five years

tin
they have
im not complaining

joanna
good to hear

tin
and in those five years ive seen my colleagues rise to higher ranks
in those five years my counterparts have risen to better and higher jobs
i now have superiors who have spent less than half the time i have at this
company

joanna
so whats the point

tin
i thought this was going to be my time
brett phillips has only been here two years jo
the other night in bed-

joanna
i told you never to talk about that here

tin
im sorry
but if im good enough for you in bed
i should be good enough here

joanna
youre treading a fine line

tin
just listen to me please
the other night
you said you would consider me

joanna
i thought you were joking

tin
why would i be joking
what can brett phillips do that i cant as well
why would you not consider me for this promotion

joanna
they would laugh
if i even suggested it in the meetings
they would laught at the thought of –

                              an outburst
tin
the thought of what
im smarter than half the people you've promoted before me
im a harder worker
im diligent
im here on time
i work extra hours
i listen and i am attentive
why am i not in charge now
explain it to me
im fucking tired-

joanna
DON'T TALK TO ME THAT WAY
                              silence
                    silence
                         silence
              hes never spoken to anyone this way
tin
im sorry
im exhausted

joanna
you don't have what it takes

tin
what it takes

joanna
im going to tell you this because i like you
off the record
you are just not a leader
the people who lead these companies are tigers
they are tigers that make even the most powerful tremble before them
they are people to be feared
they are people you do not cross
they are people whos eyes you do not look at directly
like the sun because they might burn you with one simple gaze
like medusa because you might become nothing but stone in front of them
they command presence
they command respect
does this sound like you

tin
i mean

joanna
DOES
THIS
SOUND
LIKE
YOU

tin
i work hard

joanna
i didn't think so

tin
are you saying this is where im going to be the rest of my life

joanna
most of the company doesn't even know your name
and the ones who do
don't even say it right
they call you TIM
TIM
and you never even correct them

tin
i didn't want to insult them

joanna
being what you are is fine tin
youre not a tiger
youre a worker bee
but youre an excellent worker bee
be proud of that

tin
so this is the end of the line for me

joanna
no one takes you for a leader tin
you don't speak up in meetings
you don't present new ideas

tin
that's because i listen
that is how i show respect

joanna
well your respect is not getting you anywhere

tin
so this is it
this is what the company thinks

joanna
im telling you as a friend
okay
i have a meeting i need to get to

tin
okay

joanna
ill see you tonight

tin
sure

joanna
off you go

tin
joanna

joanna
yea

tin
thank you for your honesty

the sound of a bomb on the verge of going off

scene.

columbus park
a small boom box plays soothing music
calming sounds
we can still hear pieces of new york breathing
alive
luke and koren
stand facing each other in a circle
koren is pretty cool, sort of spastic and ADD breaking into song
whenever bored
shes in more practical yoga sweats and a t-shirt
luke, the ring leader, stands shirtless
they are doing tai-chi
even though they've done it before
they don't REALLY remember what theyre doing
right now theyre doing the warm up exercise making fists and hitting
their sides
oh yea, theyre high school juniors
and they speak like rapid fast
likeyouhavenoideayouknowwhatimsaying

koren
whys this bitch always late

luke
always

koren
always

koren
ohmygod luke
my aunt totally tried to add me on facebook today

luke
NO
what did you do

koren
not confirm her
obvi

luke
i confirm everyone

koren
even people you don't know

luke
yea
all press is good press

koren
what about your parents

luke
neither of them is on facebook
thank god

koren
yea its weird

luke
totally weird

> *a moment*
> *and then*
> *brandi lazily walks in*
> *shes in very form fitting pink tights and a cut off shirt*
> *head band*
> *i don't think she knows this madonna look*
> *was vintage and cool five years ago*
> *now its come and gone again- but shes often late to the party*

brandi
why aren't you wearing a shirt

luke
i forgot my other shirt at home and i don't want to get this one all sweaty

brandi
i don't believe you

luke
shut up brandi
its not like hes fat or anything

brandi
fuck off koren
nobody asked you
hes just trying to show off

luke
so what if i am

koren
its not a bad view

luke
thanks koren

koren
youre welcome baby

brandi
you guys disgust me

luke
quit being a bitch and breath out your mouth

koren
i always forget to breathe

brandi
who are you showing off for

luke
none of your business

brandi
tell me

luke
no

koren
don't tell her luke

brandi
koren

koren
its more fun to watch her squirm

brandi
no fair you guys
this isn't how BFF's treat each other

luke
nope

brandi
come on please

luke
you always get all jealous and shit

koren
mad jealous

brandi
not true

luke
you get all competitive
and like try to take things that aren't yours

koren
yea like a vulture

brandi
a what

luke
a vulture
you know a bird

brandi
i know what a vulture is you bitch
why am i like a vulture

koren
cuz your always like scavenging
like taking other peoples shit
and like saying its yours
like making it yours
or something

brandi
nah ah

koren
like the time you tried to tell everyone you discovered patti smith
even though everyone had already been reading that book

brandi
i gave that book to daniella

koren
right
or like how i got my nails done at that place in soho and then the next day you did too

brandi
we're BFF's
imitation is the biggest form of flattery

luke
except when you take credit for it

koren
or like how you tried to lay claim on derek

brandi
fuck you

luke
shouldn't have brought that up k

koren
ohmygod its been like a year
like get over it already

brandi
that bitch stole my man

koren
except she didn't

brandi
she totally did
at the end of last year
right before summer
this bitch vivienne
this bitch VI-VI-ENNE
didn't even look up
didn't even bat an eye
this bitch
my BFF
my best friend forever
your sister
totally hears me
LUKE

luke
what

brandi
you were there

luke
she did

brandi
i did
see
i did

koren
its not stealing if it aint yours
he picked her

brandi
koren
you are working my last nerve
i cant believe youre going to take her side over mine

koren
i didn't pick no one
im here aren't i

brandi
alright Switzerland

koren
youre just mad vivienne won
she always wins

brandi
bitch i will shank you

koren
your tiny white ass
please

luke
should we do some stretches now

koren
you guys
i don't think this works very well

brandi
yea
i don't feel centered or at peace or anything

luke
that's cuz you bitches haven't stopped talking since we started
youre supposed to be quiet

> *they are quiet for a moment*
> *and then*
> *koren sings a line or two from a contemporary song*
> *its like rihanna or alicia keys or janet*
> *maybe shes really really old school giving you some whitney*

houston

> *shes really, really good*

luke
silence koren

koren
sorry
sometimes it just happens
the song is in me you know
and it needs to come out
it begs to be heard
i cant ignore the impulses

luke
will you just control yourself

koren
ill try
ill shut up

luke
good

koren
but only if you promise

luke
promise what

koren
to take me to that bar
where they have the karaoke

luke
winnies

koren
yes

luke
koren again

koren
please
i cant help myself

luke
i don't know

koren
come on

luke
fine

koren
thank you boo boo

> *a moment of silence*
> *and then it is broken*
> *brandi sings a piece of a song BADLY*
> *and you know, its something like totally lame*
> *like ke$ha or taylor swift*
> *or like nicki minaj*

luke
what. the. fuck.
i will choke you in your sleep

> *she doesn't stop*

luke
brandi
BRANDI

koren
this bitch has gone up and lost her mind

luke
BRANDI

> *she stops*

luke
thank you

brandi
tell me who it is
tell me who it is
tell me who it is
come on
tell me who youre showing off for
tellmewhoitis
tellmewhoitis
tell me who it is and ill stop
ill stop
ill stop

luke
FINE
its kaelan

brandi
KAELAN
WHOS KAELAN

luke
shut up brandi
don't yell his name
why don't you fuckin tweet about it
jesus

brandi
sorry
whos kaelan

luke
graduated two years ago kaelan

brandi
HOT KAELAN

luke
BRANDI

koren
shouldn't have told her

brandi
shut up koren

koren
im just sayin

brandi
you aint saying shit
he is so hot

koren
its all that weight he lost
remember when he used to be fat

brandi
that was a long time ago

luke
i don't know
hes like so confident
like hes got swagger or something

brandi
yea i guess so
id toss it at him

koren
see
you shouldn't have said shit

brandi
what
its not like he can have him or anything
hes straight

luke
well

brandi
WELL
what have you heard

luke
i thinks hes like bi now
or something
i don't know

brandi
that's so cool

like me

koren
you are not bi brandi

brandi
except for that time we hooked up

koren
we didn't hook up
we made out
and it was once
when we were drunk

brandi
whatever
youre so narrow minded
trying to box me in
telling me i cant be who i am

luke
youre not bi brandi

brandi
you don't know
you don't know anything
my identity is fluid
i am discovering who i am

koren
more like ripping off everyone else

brandi
what bitch

koren
fine brandi
youre bi
we'll get you a sticker

brandi
lick my cooch

koren
you wish

brandi
so how do you know

luke
i don't know
i think he was maybe flirting with me
at the record store

brandi
wait
i thought he went to stanford
this is so confusing

luke
he dropped out
moved back
and now works at the record store

brandi
people don't work in record stores

koren
he does

brandi
that's like gross or something

luke
whats gross

brandi
you cant like date somebody who works in a record store
fuck him maybe
but date
no
that's like
so
that's like not classy
that's like
so lower class
youre like better than that
might as well date someone who works at fucking starbucks or something

luke
shut up brandi

koren
yea brandi
youre being a total bitch

brandi
im just saying what we're all thinking
he works in a record store
he cant support you
hes not going anywhere
hes like unmotivated and apathetic

luke
shut up brandi
youre a spoiled white bitch
whos mom pays for everything
you can only afford to talk shit
cuz your mom wipes your ass for you with money
don't judge him
what do you know
you've never had a job
you've never worked for anything
you don't know
youre just like spoiled and mean

brandi
i volunteer at the shelter with my mom on weekends

luke
big fuckin whoop
want a medal

brandi
im just saying

luke
and how do you know hes unmotivated
he wants to be a musician

brandi
he and every other bitch in brooklyn
might as well date some broke actors who serves tables

luke
thanks for the support

brandi
im just looking out for you boo boo

you know that

a moment

luke
i know

brandi
i love you

luke
sorry i called you a spoiled white bitch

brandi
its okay
i am

luke
im a spoiled white bitch too

brandi
only half
so he flirted with you

luke
yea i think so
and then

brandi
what

luke
i like did research
i like asked around about him

koren
girl you are moving quick

luke
so i heard

brandi
what
what

luke
i don't know
i just heard that like when he drinks

he gets like more "open" or something

brandi
SEE
like me
i am bi
ohmygod
drinking makes you bi

koren
shut up brandi

brandi
so what are you gonna do about it

luke
about what

brandi
kaelan duh

luke
nothing

brandi
what do you mean nothing

luke
im like shy okay
im like shy and shit
leave me alone

brandi
you gotta toss it at him
don't be a pussy

luke
fuck you brandi

brandi
fine
if you don't
then i will

koren
THIS TRICK
luke didn't i say

what did i say

brandi
what
if hes not gonna do anything about it
he'll just end up like wasted unused goods
and that's like lame

koren
five minutes ago he wasn't shit
and now hes unused goods

luke
shut up shut up
shut up
hes here
hes here
and hes like looking
hes like looking over here
do the next move

                            they all awkwardly move into a different stretch
          or side
               they all
      end up going
              in different
                        directions

luke
fuck
we look like morons
oh shit
oh shit
oh shit oh shit oh shit

koren
what

brandi
what

koren
what

luke
hes coming over here

koren
shit

brandi
fuck

luke
act cool act cool
                                    kaelan approaches them
                                        hes wearing skinny jeans and boots
                            white t.... maybe a black Henley
kaelan
what are you guys doing

luke
tai chi

kaelan
cool

brandi
yea
lukes like people do it you know
so we took a class

kaelan
your people

brandi
the Koreans

luke
we're chinese brandi

brandi
but the karaoke bar

luke
is Korean
but im chinese

brandi
how was i supposed to know

luke
never mind

koren
its really cool
it like makes your body feel good
im koren
this is brandi
worked out and stuff
but like puts you at peace
right guys

brandi
totally

luke
at peace
right

kaelan
looks cool

luke
you should try it sometime

kaelan
yea maybe
ive been working out more

luke
yea
i noticed
we noticed

brandi
its been a long time
you look really good

koren
BRANDI

kaelan
thanks
youre looing pretty good too

brandi
thanks

luke
thanks

kaelan
oh
you too
brandi

awkward

koren
so do you have any plans tonight

kaelan
me

koren
yea
friday night

kaelan
thinking of going to a movie

koren
lukes having people over at his house

brandi
you are

koren
yea

luke
totally
you should come

kaelan
yea

koren
lukes got beer and everything

brandi
you do

luke
i do

koren
you should definitely come over

kaelan
sounds like a plan

luke
awesome
yea
great
ill facebook you

kaelan
ill see you tonight

and hes off

luke
oh my god

brandi
oh my god

koren
oh my god
i am like the best wing woman ever

brandi
you are so totally getting laid tonight

luke
fuck
what am i gonna do
i don't have beer at my house

koren
i can steal a six pack from my parents

brandi
is that enough beer for all of us

koren
we're not going brandi

brandi
why not

koren
do you wanna be a cock block

brandi
oh yea right

luke
but what am i gonna tell kaelan

koren
ouch

luke
what

she coughes

koren
i think i have a cold

luke
what about brandi

brandi
yea what about brandi

koren
shes coming over and feeding me chicken soup

brandi
i am

koren
you are
we can have our own six pack

luke
nice

brandi
nice

koren
good session

luke
yea
tai chi is awesome

scene.

the family living room
it is a well appointed apartment
clean, classy, upscale, tasteful

vivienne is playing the violin
its beautiful but sad and harsh
she plays for a few minutes
and then
there is a knock at the door
she doesn't hear it at first
and then the knock happens again
still she doesn't hear it
and then the knock gets louder
and louder
and LOUDER
startled
she scratches on the violin
she sets it aside and goes to the door and opens it
the old fashioned traveling salesman stands at the door
he is tall, lean, well dressed and dapper
this man
well he is not your every day traveling salesman
he is wearing a dark purple suit
more opening night at the MET ball than salesman
he wears fabulous shoes-
maybe they are suede or have a heel
his hair is slicked back and he has a huge grin on his face
in his hand he holds a beautiful, classy suitcase with an imprinted
logo on it
this shit is fierce and high class emerald city style
everything about this man is precise
his movement, his speech, his expressions are all purposeful and
flawless
he does this a lot
and more importantly
he does it well

vivienne
can i help you

traveling salesman
good evening
im here to see miss wood

vivienne
she is still at work

traveling salesman
i am not here to see julie ann wood
on the faculty of so and so university
whos train arrives in precisely thirty three minutes and fifty two seconds
i am here to see miss vivienne wood

vivienne
there must be some mistake

traveling salesman
there are never any mistakes miss

vivienne
did the doorman let you up

traveling salesman
that's right

vivienne
he didn't buzz me

traveling salesman
he was expecting me
im making house calls in the building today
door to door
we are part of the same union your doorman and i

vivienne
okay

traveling salesman
may i come in

vivienne
my mother isn't here

traveling salesman
im here for you

vivienne
i think theres been-

traveling salesman
we never make mistakes
vivienne wood
middle names west

mother had an affinity for the designer
slid into a swarm of bees on your fourth birthday
at the park not knowing they would not be happy about it
you still remember those stings don't you
i have in my records that you love elephants
have always wanted to get lost in a jungle on safari
dear girl
the violin is like nails on a chalk board to you
and you dream of enjoying juicy mangos on a summer day far from here
but a great journey still needs to happen before that can occur
we
make
no
mistakes
may i come in
i have another appointment shortly

vivienne
sure
                    he comes in
traveling salesman
my name is

                    but whenever he says his name all we hear is static
                            or an old song
                                or a sharp chord
                                    or silence
                    even though he is clearly saying it
traveling salesman
of the old league of traveling salesman

vivienne
excuse me

traveling salesman
miss

vivienne
i didn't catch your name

traveling salesman
my name is
                    and it happens again
traveling salesman
of the old league of traveling salesman

vivienne
that's odd

traveling salesman
ah yes
as time moves forward things begin to change
new things replace old things
we at the old league believe in direct connection
high quality service
and personal warnings

vivienne
warnings

traveling salesman
i am here today to talk to you about life insurance

vivienne
life insurance

traveling salesman
you are repeating almost everything i am saying miss
are you some kind of parrot

vivienne
no

traveling salesman
didn't think so
carrying on then
i am here to talk to you about coming up with the best plan for you
it is smarter to purchase these plans sooner than later

vivienne
i don't need life insurance

traveling salesman
everyone needs life insurance

vivienne
i think this is something my parents would take care of

traveling salesman
it is not something to be done by parents im afraid
the commitment and the purchase price need to be settled on
and arranged by you alone
you and your insurance agent

me

vivienne
i think ill talk it over with my parents and contact you later

traveling salesman
im afraid it doesn't work that way
we travel you see
and once i leave
i might not be able to come back
not for a long
long time miss
and by then
well
by then it could be too late
something could have happened by the time i get around

vivienne
happened
what could have happened
                    as the list grows he gets more and more menacing
            more manic
                    like the seams are falling apart
traveling salesman
your heel could break sending you plunging down a metal staircase snapping
your neck
some petty little creature of the night could come out of the darkness
trying to steal your purse and take you away with it
a meteorite could crash through that window tainted with an chemical
turning you into a monster
a tiny little needle could take arms against you and sew you into the bottom of the
past
left could turn into right
water could become fire and east could become west
car accident
dog bite
snake bite
food poison
blood poison
cancer
crabs
syphilis
a thousand little things could happen right outside that door miss
be smart
invest in your future
protect yourself against life

vivienne
i don't understand

he suddenly becomes cool, calm, and collected

traveling salesman
life miss
many things could happen at any single moment
we are here to protect you against them
for the right price

vivienne
please get out

traveling salesman
im only trying to help you miss
name the right sacrifice
find the right price
its how life works
in order to get something
you must invest something

vivienne
thank you for stopping by
but i don't need your help

traveling salesman
trust me
you do
for whats coming

vivienne
whats coming

traveling salesman
the future miss
life

vivienne
id like you to go now please

traveling salesman
very well

he gets up and walks to the door

vivienne
sorry
thank you for stopping by

traveling salesman
miss

vivienne
yes

traveling salesman
it is you who is going to be sorry
please take this
my card
most likely
the next time i see you
the price will be too high

she does so
vivienne
thank you

traveling salesman
good evening miss

vivienne
good evening

and he vanishes

scene.

a karaoke bar- winnies
low, red lighting
sort of dingy, sort of campy, sort of hilarious
luke, brandi, and koren sit at a booth
sounds of really bad karaoke in the background

luke
thanks for the six pack koren

koren
of course
youre my bitch
you know id pull through

brandi
why do we always have to come here

koren
cuz its hilarious
and im always the best singer in the room

luke
kore is it your turn yet

koren
im next

luke
good i have to go home soon

koren
for kaelan

luke
for kaelan

koren
for kaelan

brandi
did you guys see alicia ross today
she was all flirting with Brandon
wearing that tiny little scarf things as a dress
doesn't she know
she doesn't even like fit into it
her tits all popping out

like what a skank right
i heard that shes like telling people that she wants to go to prom with him
that shes hoping that he'll ask her
like yea right
like yea fucking right
like he would ever ask her out
like she would ever look good with him
like people would ever believe that they like belong or whatever
some people
some people have no perspective outside of themselves
some people just cant see what everyone else can
fucking alicia ross
and brandon
yea right
yea fucking right
im going to prom with him
not her
not her
shes all
shes all
shes all trying to get in my way
i took care of it
i took care of it
bitch had it coming

luke
what did you do

brandi
did you hear she got herpes from that dude she was fucking from queens
fucking queens

koren
what dude

brandi
you know what dude
this is why you don't fuck dudes from queens

luke
she was fucking some dude from queens

brandi
yep

koren
alicia ross

really
i coulda sworn she was all prudish and shit

brandi
nope

koren
wow
you coulda fooled me

luke
alicia ross
herpes
rough

brandi
and that ladies is how you start a rumor
that is how you take a bitch down

koren
are you serious

brandi
once you put it out there
you cant take it back
people will believe anything

koren
you are so cray cray sometimes
on the real real
cray cray

somes calls korens name: KORn

koren
oh its my turn!
im next
its koREN

koren goes up to the microphone

luke
seriously b
you can be so fucked up sometimes

brandi
don't give me that look
don't judge me
now im a bitch
i wasn't a bitch when i took down marc foster for calling you a faggot last year
cuz you were too much of a bitch to do it yourself

that's the difference between you and i luke
i always gotta do the dirty work
the rest of you just stand aside and reap the benefits
and where were you when everyone was a bitch to me before
in kindergarten when sarah fogel called me a fat cow
or when lauren weems spit in my face
or when jake nguyen told everyone i gave bad head
i don't remember where you were
keeping you distance
well you know what
im not at the bottom anymore luke
im not
im not
ive clawed my way to the top
and im staying up here
and im not feeling bad about it
not one bit
NOT
ONE
BIT

luke
okay

brandi
that's what i thought

she giggles and kisses his cheek
and then koren is on the mic

koren
this song is for my BFF's brandi and luke

brandi and luke cheer
koren starts to sing "i will always love you" – whitney
huoston version
or maybe its "i have nothing"
either way
its serious
but just when the song is about to climax
there is a
BLACKOUT
a few gasps and "whats going on" and "boos"
are heard
koren
is this another black out
mother fucking new york city
whys shit always breaking down on me

95

scene.

luke, kaelan, and vivienne sit on the floor of lukes room
he has posters of new order on his wall
joy division and the strokes
maybe the breakfast club or st. elmos
fire
his room is pretty organized
books, records, everything is meticulous

they are playing liars dice
they shake the cups
SLAM!
they laugh
they go around
maybe twice if its fast

vivienne
okay guys
this has to be the last round for me

luke
come on you owe me

kaelan
but we're having so much fun

vivienne
i have to talk to mom

kaelan
hey
maybe we can crack open some of those beers you mentioned
and listen to music or
something

vivienne
what beers

luke
kaelan

kaelan
oh shit sorry
was that
was that
should i have kept my mouth shut about that

vivienne
YOU HAVE BEER UP HERE

luke
keep your voice down

vivienne
its against the law

kaelan
i brought them over

vivienne
what

kaelan
yea
i

vivienne
i thought you said he-

kaelan
no i did
and asked him to stash it

vivienne
luke you've been drinking

luke
youre making me look like an asshole viv

vivienne
well you are an asshole

luke
i cover for you all the time

vivienne
yea and youre a dick about it

luke
please viv

kaelan
be cool viv
come on

we wont go out
we're not cruising around and doing shit
we'll be up here
just listening to music
being chill
no big deal
nothings going to happen

vivienne
kaelan

luke
please viv
                    mouthing just to her:
luke
(don't ruin this for me)

vivienne
alright fine

kaelan
awesome

luke
thanks
thanks

vivienne
but if you get caught
i didn't know anything about it

kaelan
scouts honor

vivienne
i cant believe im doing this

                    she leaves
kaelan
dude that was so close
i almost blew it
                    a moment
kaelan
you wanna put on a record or something

luke
i don't have a record player remember

kaelan
oh yea
that's right
hold on

kaelan goes over to a large duffel
and pull out
an old record player

kaelan
surprise

luke
are you crazy

kaelan
i got a new one recently
so my old one was just like collecting dust under my bed
it needed a loving home
thought you could have it

luke
youre like
that's like
thanks kaelan

kaelan
and

luke
theres more

kaelan
your first record

kaelan pulls out the joy division record

luke
youre really nice
youre thoughtful

kaelan
don't mention it
wanna get the beer while i put this on

luke
yea
okay

kaelan
cool

luke fishes the beer from under his bed
or the closet
or the bottom of a drawer
does he have anything to open it with?
kaelan puts on the record
a moment
kaelan dances to the music
its mellow and cute and cool
luke just watches him
light and shadow and young love fill the air

kaelan pulls out his keys and opens the beers
maybe he does the lighter trick

luke
that's cool

kaelan
never seen someone do that before

luke
nope
it's a neat trick

kaelan
you aint seen nothing yet
im full of em
cheers

they clink bottles and drink

luke
sorry everyone else isn't here

kaelan
its cool luke

luke
yea

kaelan
yea

luke
good

kaelan
so that's cool that your parents are okay with you being gay

luke
yea
theyre
its very strange

kaelan
what is

luke
theyre very progressive
i came out when i was fourteen

kaelan
ballsy

luke
when i told my mom
all she said was
make sure hes successful and will take care of you

kaelan
they sound pretty cool your parents
very modern

luke
my mother is chinese
and my father is from connecticut
oddly enough hes the softer one

kaelan
theyre hard on you

luke
as long as we get straight A's
we can do whatever we want

kaelan
my parents don't give a shit what i do

luke
must be nice
that kind of freedom

kaelan
sometimes
sometimes the freedom is nice

sometimes the loneliness can be overwhelming
sometimes not having someone looking over your shoulder

luke
breathing down your neck

kaelan
paying attention to you

luke
controlling every move like a chess game

kaelan
holding your hand through the tough shit

luke
forcing your hand into every choice

kaelan
offering advice to progress in the right direction

luke
telling you there is only one way to live

kaelan
correcting all the mistakes they made by making sure you don't repeat them

luke
not letting you breathe

kaelan
making sure you don't drown
i didn't have that
sometimes that
that reminds you that you matter to someone
that someone cares about you and they care about your
your survival

luke
that kind of love comes with a price

kaelan
when you fall

luke
sometimes they don't catch you

kaelan
must be-

> *luke kisses kaelan*
>> *a brief moment*
>>> *and then kaelan pushes him away*

kaelan
take it easy

luke
sorry

kaelan
no
its just

luke
what

kaelan
give me some time to breathe

luke
okay

> *kaelan pops another beer*
>> *raises it to the air in a sign of cheers to luke who nods*

his head

>> *and then he swallows*
>>> *one*
>>>> *long*
>>>>> *gulp*

scene.

vivienne addresses her mother
we don't really see her mother
maybe we just see her shadow on the floor
maybe she and vivienne stand in silhouette
maybe viviennes mother is a puppet
either way
we do not see her in the flesh
but we hear her breathing
feel her reacting
and i cant say its very nice

vivienne
mom
okay
mother
i mean
i have to tell you something
its important
i think i know where im going to school
i got in
i got in to
ucla calarts
wesleyan
nyu
dartmouth
amherst
vasser
cal
williams
brown
university of chicago
yes i know
i know you think those are all easy ones
mother i
mother i
i want to go to calarts
i got a scholarship
no its
but its
its very prestigious
its
its what i want
photography
its what i want
what
harvard

yes
i did
i did hear back
i
i
i didn't get in

         suddenly a terrifying sound
      as viviennes mother slaps her across the face
           once
               then twice
     then a third time
       then a fourth
            silence
            silence
            silence
     then in a raspy, almost inhuman voice
      we hear the voice of her mother

the tiger
how dare you shame me
how dare you shame me
      and then she slaps her again
        she starts to stalk away
   a moment

vivienne
by the way mother
might as well tell you now
because youre such a good mother
your son is upstairs getting drunk underneath your nose
just thought you should know

      a terrifying growl
       and then
   a blackout

scene.

at school
two days later- monday
derek and vivienne at school

derek
i respect my family too much
they are too important to me
i would do anything for them
everything

vivienne
how can you do everything for someone who would turn their back on you
in the drop of a hat

derek
its about respect
its about doing whats right
its what i most inherited

vivienne
inherited

derek
each of us is born during the year of a certain animal
and we inherit that animals traits
i was born under the year of the boar
and i am proud of that vivienne

vivienne
what am i

derek
a rat

vivienne
gross
its not a very sexy animal
but neither is a boar

derek
maybe not
but the boar represents strength
unbreakable strength that cannot be overcome
honesty as well
most importantly they are brave
and hate to quarrel

vivienne
i don't believ that
that everyone born the same year has the same qualities
it doesn't make sense

derek
you don't have to believe it for it to be true

vivienne
it doesn't matter
love and respect are not the same thing
i choose love

derek
even if it means sacrificing everything

vivienne
well its done now
she'll never forgive me
my father is disappointed
i can see it in his eyes

derek
she will forgive you
i know it

vivienne
its not her im worried about derek
its me
       he writes something on her hand
vivienne
whats that mean

derek
it's the kanji symbol for forgiveness

vivienne
by the time she realizes ill be long gone
by the time she realizes itll be too late
ill carry this with me forever

derek
in japanese we have a saying
       he speaks a japanese phrase

vivienne
what does that mean

derek
it is better to travel hopefully
thant to arrive disenchanted

vivienne
maybe ill leave early
start school in the summer
say so long
shes a beast
teach me another saying

derek
im not a fortune cookie full of cheap wisdom

vivienne
yes you are

derek
you have to earn it then

vivienne
come on
im sad
make me feel better

he kisses her
vivienne
what happened to her to turn her into such a beast
i don't understand

derek
there is no way to understand everything

vivienne
is that another one

derek
no

vivienne
come on
teach me one more

derek
okay
ready

vivienne
ready

> *derek speaks a japanese phrase*
>> *it is a like a piece of music that hangs in the air*
> *vivienne attempts to repeat it*
close
>> *they do it together one time*

vivienne
what does it mean

derek
unless you enter the tigers den
you cant take the cubs

scene.

> *luke*
>> *brandi*
>>> *and koren*
>>>> *skyping*
>>> *they each listen to soothing sounds at home*
>> *they are in their tai chi outfits*

luke
w'ere sitting their
on my bed
hes had two beers
ive had one
and ive like never had alcohol before
so im like feeling pretty good already
and hes looking at me all like
all like
his smile
and his eyes are like just looking at me
and we're laughing cuz we're like buzzed
and that song is playing in the background

> *he sings a joy division song*
>> *its kinda cliché*
> *then koren sings the song and its really great*

brandi
i love that song

luke
right
we're like
the mood is like
like

brandi
perfect

luke
perfect
and im totally freaking out
and im totally excited
cuz its kaelan burke
and hes this close to me
THIS CLOSE

> *he demonstrates*

brandi
wow
that's hot
that so hot

luke
and i totally have a boner

koren
you did

luke
totally

koren
like a half
like a little hello chub
like just waking up from a nap
all groggy eyed to say hello
or like for real real
like lets do this

luke
full on jet setter

brandi
whoa
what about him what about him

luke
i mean i don't know

brandi
you didn't touch it

koren
we deliver you the goods
i wrap them up all nice and shiny with a little bow on top
all you gotta do is unwrap it

luke
i mean i was nervous
and i was about to
but i was like scared or whatever
but i was like rubbing his back
his shoulders
and i knew

brandi
oh for sure

koren
yea at this point

luke
and right when im about to
mother
she storms in
she motherfucking
my motherfucking would have left me alone all night had my bitch ass sister not
punked me
my mother
just barges in

brandi
barges

koren
ive had that happen

brandi
embarrassing

koren
the worst

luke
THE WORST

brandi
then what happens

koren
this is too much

luke
she rips me off him and grabs me by both arms and yells
BEER
BEER
BEER
YOU DARE BRING BEER INTO THIS HOUSE

brandi
oh shit

koren
youre like totes fucked

brandi
FUCKED

koren
did you pee yourself
i would have
i would have totally peed myself

luke
and kaelan
is like on the floor
hes like cowering in the corner or something
and hes all like
its my fault
and like im sorry i didn't know
and im like oh shit oh shit oh shit
i thought she was going to rip my face off
she looked at him and said GET OUT
and like a total
like a total fuckin movie
like some michael bay steven spielberg joint
im like
RUN
like RUN like motherfuckin run
you guys it was the worst
and its all because of fucking vivienne

brandi
told you she was a bitch

koren
she totally hated on you

brandi
ruined your life

koren
her own brother

brandi
that's cold

koren
even i didn't think vivi could get down like that
cock block
just cock destroyed you

luke
that's not all

brandi
no wait
theres more

koren
this is like totally stressful you guys

luke
my mom grounded me

brandi
for how long

luke
one month for each beer that she found

koren
fuck you

luke
fuck me is right

brandi
youre grounded for six months

koren
youre grounded for the whole summer

luke
the whole summer

brandi
so no trip to six flags on my birthday

luke
nope

koren
no going to the museum of modern art

luke
exactly

brandi
no looking at cute boys in tank tops in central park

luke
don't even bring that up

koren
its like we're all grounded

luke
no summer romance with kaelan

brandi
this is going to be the worst summer ever

> *brandi shuts her music off*
> *silence*
> *silence*

brandi
these sounds are not relaxing

koren
no they are not

luke
i do not feel mellow

brandi
i totally don't feel relaxed
but you know what IS relaxing

luke
what

brandi
payback

scene.

vivienne is at home
she is reading
and listening to classical music
a knock at the door
she opens it
the traveling salesman is back

vivienne
what are you doing here

traveling salesman
as summer approaches
the end of a season
we thought itd be nice
to sell our insurance for a very special price

vivienne
i said i don't want it

traveling salesman
you don't even know how much it costs

vivienne
why would i want to insure something that is barely worth anything

traveling salesman
we only understand the value of what we have
once we've lost it
we only know the worth of something close to us
when it is gone
vanished into thin air
as if it never existed
you are young and think have little to lose
but that which you most need
you will find is lost when most desired
a few simple pennies
some easy demands
take it from me miss
danger approaches

vivienne
okay
how much will it cost

traveling salesman
not how much
but what

vivienne
okay what

he whispers into her ear

vivienne
no
i would never
i would never do that

traveling salesman
a simple price for what you are insuring

vivienne
get out of my house

traveling salesman
you protect that which does not value you

vivienne
please leave

traveling salesman
dear girl
would he not take this offer
you or your brother
your brother future
that's all im asking
your brother future
before he takes yours
it's a simple exchange

vivienne
no
no
no
he wouldn't

traveling salesman
are you sure
are you sure
are you sure
are you sure
are you sure
simple insurance can protect you

vivienne

i am
i am
GET OUT

traveling salesman
suit yourself
don't say i didn't warn you
next time
you wont be able to afford the price

and he is gone

scene.

luke and brandi
they are in viviennes room
koren keeps watch in the hallway
shes singing old school janet

luke
hurry up

brandi
are you sure shes not going to catch us in here

luke
korens keeping watch
besides
vivienne likes to take long baths
it allows her to think or something
clear her mind

brandi
i bet shes just touching herself
that's what i do

luke
gross

brandi
im serious

luke
i don't want to think about your vagina
and i certainly don't want to talk about my sisters

brandi
im just saying

luke
can you tell me what we're looking for please
what does it look like

brandi
paper you idiot
it's a piece of scrap paper

luke
i know its paper
but is it in a notebook

a box
what do girls hide things in

brandi
i feel like
a book

luke
what

brandi
i think she stuck it in a book

luke
shes got a ton of books

brandi
okay let me think
we were
i remember we were in central park
she was studying as usual
and i was making this list right
and i told vivienne
i was like you should make one too
and she was all like no that's so stupid
and i was like no its totally fun and hilarious and like who cares
and she was like no
and finally she stopped studying
she got tired and started reading
she started reading
what the fuck was she reading
atlas fucking shrugged
find atlas shrugged

> *they go through viviennes books*
> *there are some on her dresser*
> *there are some on a little bookshelf mounted on the wall*
> *there are books on the windowsill*
> *there are a ton of books*
> *they dig through them*

luke
i got it

brandi
you did

luke

no wait i cant read
im a moron
keep looking

brandi
no
no
no
no

luke
a giant shakespeare anthology

brandi
fuck that guy
that's like not even english
that's like a whole other language

luke
not this one
no

brandi
found it
found it
i found –

luke
stop screaming
she'll hear you
open the book
open the book

> *she flips through the book until a piece of paper*
> *falls from the sky*
> *like really*
> *not from the book*
> *but like magically falls from the sky*
> *like a present*
> *it floats in a dim red light*
> *or purple maybe*
> *and lands at their feet*
> *luke grabs it and begins to unfold*

brandi
bingo

> *the sound of something shattering*

or the sound of all the air from the world being sucked out

scene.

tin appears
he is in a suit
he talks to the audience

tin
hello
hi
its good to be here
its good to be back at stuy

a long silent moment

tin
its been ten years since i graduated
so it is an honor to speak to you here today
i know im not kevin mitchell
but as you might have heard he recently became CEO of of
you know
so he had to cancel last minute
and i am
i am his replacement
replace
but
so
thank you principal lee for asking me to come back
for thinking so highly of me
thank
thank you

he pulls out a sheet of paper

tin
stuyvesant class of two thousand thirteen
welcome-
WELCOME
to the future
to your future
and what
what a beautiful future it is

he stops

tin
i had this speech all planned out
i was supposed to come back and tell you how great everything is
how after you leave high school
the world will open up for you
as it did for me
with opportunity
with potential

with potential
all the potential in the world
to change everything
to create
to make a difference
i was supposed to tell you that education is important
that education is everything
that after you go to yale like i did
or princeton or harvard or ucla or stanford
or wherever it is that you decide to go
that everything will open up for you
limitless
limitless
but that's not
that's not what im here to tell you
you see
i recently
i recently quit my job
a job that i had been at for almost a decade
i quit
i quit
my job
i quit my job
i am an american
but i am also asian
the two coexist
right
right
they coexist in me
together
so i thought
but what i learned
tradition
value
respect
silence
these things mean nothing to them
what they value
what we value
these things are not in sync
so what are we working for
who is to change
are we learning the right things
i am smarter than them
i know i am smarter than them
i think i am
i think

i know that if i add this and multiply that and divide it here
a meaning will be derived
but what that meaning does
what it actually means
i cannot understand it
its foreign
what about us
what about you
what about me
what about me
how much longer are we to be silence
tradition is all i know
that is all i know
and its hasn't
its killing me
what i know
what i am
what i do
what i do
what i do
i quit my
i quit my
what am i left with
who am i now

> *there is a deafening silence*

tin
i thought
i worked so hard
but i wasn't good enough
me
can anyone
can anyone help me
i have nothing
what am i
what
please
please
please
listen
cant you see
anyone

> *do people begin to boo?*
> *does someone gently try to lead him off stage?*
> *or is it just brutal silence?*

tin

125

please
don't you see
i need help
i am just a man
with so many questions
help me to understand
sorry

blackout

scene.

luke sits in the living room
he is watching a movie
mommie dearest
we hear a soundbite
THAT iconic scream
vivienne comes out of her room

vivienne
hey

silence

vivienne
im still pretty shaken up about that guy
tin
i feel so sad for him
what do you think happened to him
he went crazy
it was sad right
it was sad
luke
luke
alright
tell mom i went to the park

luke
i don't care

vivienne
ill be back before dinner

luke
nobody cares

vivienne
luke

luke
fuck off

vivienne
don't talk to me that way
i love you

luke
i said
FUCK OFF

vivienne
i made a mistake
we all make mistakes
someday you will too

luke
youll be sorry

vivienne
i already am

luke
you don't know how sorry youre going to be

vivienne
there will be other boys

luke
not like this one

vivienne
let me give you some advice-

luke
youre only a year older than me vivienne

vivienne
trust me it makes a difference

luke
tell somebody who cares

vivienne
alright
ill be back later

luke
I DON'T CARE

> *she leaves*
> *he pulls out the note and looks at it*
> *there is a knock at the door*
> *he stuffs the note back in his pocket*
> *another knock*
> *he opens the door*

luke
I SAID NO ONE CA-

> *but its not vivienne*
> *it's the traveling salesman*

luke
sorry i thought you were

traveling salesman
good evening my name is
> *but all we hear is static*
> *or an old song*
> *or a sharp chord*
> *or silence*
> *even though he is clearly saying his name*

traveling salesman
of the old league of traveling salesman
and i am here with a very special offer for a mister luke wood

> *he smiles*

scene.

the traveling salesman appears in spot
he speaks to the audience

traveling salesman
we live in troubling times
times that will only get more troubling
we tried to warn you
to slow you down
to tell you to stop
but you wouldn't listen would you
no
you wouldn't
so now we're here to make you listen
to remind you of all the things of which you are capable of
to show you what it is that you have done
and let me remind you
what you have done
not what we have
he looks at his watch

traveling salesman
oh
i think its showtime
youre on kid

he points at luke
who speaks to the audience

luke
so if everyone hasn't heard yet
im grounded for the next six months
why
because vivienne decided to rat me out
and tell my parents
about the six pack of beer i was hiding in my room
my mom is asian
and all of you know
that asian parents
are fucking strict
so six cans equals six months of being grounded
little over the top
not if your parents are asian
and your sister is a filthy bitch
since all i can do
and all ill ever do for the next five and a half months
involves sitting on the computer all day

i thought id get a little revenge today
everyone out there thinks my sister is such a sweet and innocent girl
but a few days ago
i decided to go treasure hunting in her room
with an unnamed friend
who my sister has also fucked over
and found a little something special hidden in her closet
this will make the next five and a half months bearable
ladies and gentleman my sister is a whore
i present to you her hook up list

> *does luke read this list*
> *maybe the traveling salesman does*
> *maybe the whole cast does it*
> *maybe various people appear as they are named*
> *maybe we go back in time and see the list being created*
> *or maybe just vivienne*
> *reads it alone in the cold cold light*

vivienne
one

adrian matthews
finger me
maybe hj

two

ronnie trent
blow job

three

dang tran
only kiss

four

josh taylor
finger me
hj
blow job
tittie bang
and maybe v-card

five

derek key

blow job

six

kaelan burke
v-card
but people say hes gay

seven

jacob nguyen
only kiss
if he cuts his hair
i might give him a blow job

eight

russel terra
he ate me out
awesome
i want him to make me go O

nine

nick charles
i will do anything he wants
i will do everything he wants
soooooooooo
HOT

> *silence*
> *silence*
> *silence*
> *meanwhile*
> *the traveling salesman grins*
> *and grins*
> *and grins*
> *and grins*
> *and looks at the audience*

traveling salesman
but lets not forget the flurry of responses

1
note to self
do not hook up with vivienne

2

what a whore

3
damn son

koren
oh em
gee

4
this is
so epic

kaelan
you are a dick
but this is so funny
also im not gay

5
holy shit

brandi
hey jacob
if you cut your hair youre getting a bj
hahahahahahha

derek
HOLY SHIT

6
ohem f
g

7
i love facebook

brandi
i knew she was a closet slut

koren
this is so wrong

8
tweeted it

9
instagrammed it

10
hashtag slut

11
she has some bad taste

12
this trick

13
this bitch

derek
luke
i really think you should take this down
this is so wrong on so many levels

14
CALLED OUT

15
this is so fucked up

16
i second that

17
if i could like this twice i would

and then vivienne catches wind
vivienne
TAKE THIS DOWN NOW
WHAT THE FUCK IS WRONG WITH YOU

luke
what are you gonna do
tell mom and dad that i uploaded your dick sucking list to facebook
go ahead

18
omg

kaelan
no way

vivienne
EVERYONE DE-TAG YOURSELVES NOW
REMOVE THE TAGS LUKE OR IM GOING TO SERIOUSLY HURT YOU
TAKE THIS PICTURE DOWN NOW
PICK UP YOUR PHONE

luke
i heart facebook like you heart cock

> *and then silence*
> *and everyone is looking at vivienne*
> *they are surrounding her*
> *they are circled around her*
> *staring*
> *and staring*
> *and staring*
> *and staring*
> *and staring*
> *and then*
> *a stomp*
> *stomp*
> *stomp*
> *something STOMPING towards everyone*
> *and then*
> *a GIANT TERRIFYING GROWL*

> *blackout*

END OF ACT ONE

act two.

scene.

> a sound like something exploding
> a sound like all of the air is being sucked out of the universe
> and the characters are all their
>> well all of them except for luke, vivienne, the travelsing salesman
> and the tiger
>> they look at the audience
>> in the darkness
>> and then they EXPLODE into crazy gesture mode
>> crazy
>>> schizophrenic
>>> fast and overwhelming
>> and then they all stop
>> suddenly
>> as if they've become aware of the audience
>> as if they've caught us looking in on them
>>> suddenly they all say
>> "THIS IS HOW YOU WANTED IT"
> and then they go away
>> they vanish
>> and we bleed into:

scene.

a den like a bombed out shelter in a jungle
a window covered in vines
the sound of waves crashing
trees and leaves
decaying
a window
out of this window
in the distance we see water
this den is both a complete room
but also architecturally open
we see the jungle the room is in
the jungle is all around
and breaking through

vivienne is in the corner
cold and sad and broken and alone
she has been on a very long journey here
like a great
big
long
fall

and then brandi appears
she is a vulture...
literally
she circles around vivienne
cackling

brandi
poor poor broken thing

vivienne
come to see what you've done

brandi
i can smell it from way up there
the blood
and the fear
the sadness
you reek of it
that stench
its intoxicating

vivienne
haven't you done enough

brandi
im still hungry

brandi pecks at vivienne

vivienne
get away

brandi
but youre still fresh
all that meat
ripe for the picking
would be a shame to waste

brandi pecks at vivienne
vivienne tries to push her away
but she is too weak

vivienne
what more do you want

brandi
bone
i want to slurp the marrow

she slurps

brandi
i want to get to the juicy bits

vivienne
i never did anything to you

brandi
you took away my happiness
you took from me the thing i wanted

vivienne
you can be the smartest
the fastest
the funniest
you can be the prettiest
you can have him
or her
and this and that
take it
its yours
i don't want it

brandi
you don't have to offer them to me
ill take them for myself

vivienne
just let me dwell here in
in in
in
what this is

brandi
oh
youre no fun when you don't struggle
youre weaker than i thought you were
i thought you were my equal
but youre
just
pathetic
and weak
empty hollow eyes
your eye lids sag
to the floor
like your dripping down forever
melting away
a creature made of liquid
drip
drip
drip
plop
plop
plop
a mess of wet
nothingness

vivienne
you don't know whats inside me
you don't know what i am

brandi
i can tell you this
                she pecks at vivienne
youre not like me
                  peck
youre not a majestic bird
                    peck
there are no strong feathers lining your back
                          peck
you were not made to soar
                  peck
you were not meant to spread your body in grandeur

                              peck
seeking
seeking
seeking
the sky
                    peck
but instead made to be broken
crushed on the ground
                    peck
i can see you from way up here vivienne
                              peck
do you see me

                              peck

i am waving
i am waving
i am waving
down to you
from way up here
from way up here
i am waving
from the top
from the top
waving to you
at the bottom
at the bottom
at the bottom
waving to you
                         peck
                              peck
               peck
                    but this time
                         as she goes to peck her
                    vivienne grabs brandis wings

vivienne
you are no beautiful bird brandi
you are no strong

brandi
let go of me

vivienne
or courageous
or honorable bird

brandi
youre hurting me

vivienne
you are neither song bird nor cardinal
you are no mocking bird or owl

brandi
my wings

vivienne
you don't have the vibrant colors of a flamingo or parrot

brandi
ow

vivienne
you are no raven or condor or eagle or hawk

brandi
ow

vivienne
youre nothing but
a vulture
a filthy
scrap eating
vulture
a dirty
dishonorable
vulture
i may not be a beautiful winged bird
but at least
at least
i am no vulture

vivienne
now flit off before i snap off your wings

vivienne lets brandi go
the sound of a thunderstorm approaching
brandi makes the loud jagged sound of a vulture
she flies away
a little less high than when she came in
vivienne is alone
she is lost
and alone
she starts to sing a song
the song is current
some brooklyn hipster song by GIRLS

or twin shadow
or the xx
you know the kind of song
she sings
but the song doesn't seem to come out right
she tries over and over again
she tries again but all that comes out is a cry in a different
language
the cry is like a cough
she chokes on the words and then quiets down
confused
thinking
until she starts to sing another song
one that feels familiar
yet not
the song is very old
ancient
like the one we heard in the park
an old chinese song
she sings for a moment
and then
derek wanders in
he is
a BOAR

derek
at the center of the jungle
somewhere deep down and dark
i woke up lost
i woke up twisted and entangled
blurry tongued and bloody eyed
i felt trapped in my body
my own body became my own enemy
feeling unfamiliar
this body that id known so well
this body id known so long
all id known
had turned on me and become something
unrecognizable
like a glove on the wrong foot
like a song with the wrong words kissed into your ears
by someone
by something
you used to know
so i followed the sounds
letting them lead me to a place that felt familiar
only to find
only to find

only to find
you
who are you

vivienne
vivienne

derek
you don't sound like her
you don't look like her

he kisses her

derek
you don't taste like her

vivienne
its me

derek
i don't believe you

vivienne
its still me
its me
its me

derek
things are different here
how odd

vivienne
that list

derek
that list

vivienne
that list
i wrote it a long time ago

derek
a long time ago

vivienne
before you and i even knew each other

derek
before

vivienne
before

derek
before

vivienne
before the idea of you and i was even invented
i was a different person then

derek
a different person

vivienne
just a child

derek
just a child

vivienne
you understand me right

derek
you

vivienne
right

derek
just a child

vivienne
derek

derek
sometimes things get trapped in your head
and no matter how hard you try you cant get them out
yes
no
maybe
right
what
wait

vivienne
i love you

derek
im overwhelmed by feelings
i didn't know i had
like the levee broke and all this stuff is rushing in
but love
isn't one of them

vivienne
you don't mean that

derek
i think i do

vivienne
i didn't know you could be so cold

derek
i didn't know you could be so cheap

vivienne
it was a small thing
i wrote a long time ago
when i was a freshman
just a kid
a childish thing

derek
but right now
it feels like the most important thing in the world
and right now feels like itll last forever

vivienne
nothing lasts forever

> *a moment*

derek
the image i have of you
is seered into my brain
and ill think of it
and live in it
so that next time
i wont be so foolish
i wont be so foolish

> *he starts to go*
> *a moment*

vivienne
derek

he turns around

vivienne
i didn't take you for a coward
i thought you were supposed to be brave
so much for your unbreakable strength

derek
so often things are not what you want them to be
people can be so surprising

> *and he disappears*
> *after a moment*
> *the sounds of a thunderstorm getting closer*
> *and closer*
> *and closer*
> *vivienne looks for cover*
> *and then tropical winds*
> *and rain*
> *and rain*
> *and rain*
> *the old fashioned traveling salesman appears*
> *he watches her*
> *he feels sorry for her*

traveling salesman
i told you this wouldn't end well for you

vivienne
leave me alone

traveling salesman
im the only friend you got down here

vivienne
friend
i don't even know what that word means
friend
friend
its like metal in my mouth
rotten and poisonous
i choke on the word friend

traveling salesman
you can still get out

vivienne
theres nothing for me back there

traveling salesman
that so juvenile of you

vivienne
well i am
just a juvenile

traveling salesman
you are no kid doll
at least not anymore
youre older now

vivienne
all ive learned
is that in this life
there is no winning
in this life
traps everywhere
giant bear claws meant to snap you in half
no matter what direction you run in
holes everywhere
hidden under leaves
where you cant see

traveling salesman
im going to tell you something
because i like you

vivienne
why

traveling salesman
because i like you

vivienne
why

traveling salesman
cant a person just like another person these days

vivienne
not your kind of person

traveling salesman
ouch
what you have to learn
is very simple

its very american
actually
its not even american
just a fact about the world
are you listening

vivienne
fuck off

traveling salesman
in this life everything comes with a price
everything costs something
if you want anything
you have to give something up
its as simple as that
what are you willing to risk for what you want
what will you sacrifice
evolve
evolve
evolve
youre not a child anymore
you cant have it all
you should have taken my offer

vivienne
i couldn't

traveling salesman
your brother is the reason youre down here

vivienne
well i don't believe in revenge

                              giant growling sounds are heard in the distance
traveling salesman
suit yourself
this is the last youll see of me
                              he starts to go
vivienne
wait
what about her

traveling salesman
who knows what she has planned for you
but you have a lifetime to find out
                              a moment
                       and then

vivienne
you can have him
whatever he was meant to be
the life he was meant to lead

traveling salesman
im sorry

vivienne
now what

traveling salesman
that deals no longer on the table

vivienne
but what
i thought

traveling salesman
that's the thing about insurance
if you wait
the price can change
your brother already made his own deal with me
hes very impulsive

vivienne
what did he

traveling salesman
oh im sorry
customer salesman privilege
you know how it is

vivienne
so that's it

traveling salesman
im afraid so

vivienne
just me and her then

traveling salesman
well there is

vivienne
what

traveling salesman
no
never mind
i couldn't

vivienne
tell me

traveling salesman
there is another way

> *he gets close to her and opens his mouth*
> *and then the deafening noise*
> *the static*
> *the overwhelming*

vivienne
what if i don't

traveling salesman
its only if
> *she thinks*

vivienne
if i accept your proposition

traveling salesman
ill take care of her

vivienne
i accept

traveling salesman
stay still and quiet
and don't say a word
> *he points to another corner*
> *and luke appears*

luke
hello
> *and then the roar of a tiger*

luke
mom
> *and then all of a sudden*
> *stuff*
> *flies*
> *through*
> *the air*
> *like its being tossed*

its coming from a dark corner
>*stuff is being flung out the window*
>*onto the water below*

shoes
>*books*
>>*pictures*
>*sweaters*
>>>*love*

memories
>*cardboard cutouts*
>*the stuff that makes a life*

luke
mom
mom what are you doing
mom is that my
is that my stuff
what are you doing
what are you doing
>*luke sees the traveling salesman*
>*maybe he runs to him and grabs his arm*
>>*maybe he just tries to wave him down*
>*either way*
>>*hes trying to get his attention*
>>>*desperately*

luke
i thought you were helping me

traveling salesman
i am

luke
but look

traveling salesman
oh im sorry
i have nothing to do with that
not
a
thing

luke
youre leaving

traveling salesman
oh ill be back
to collect
we always do

and he vanishes
leaving luke alone
because that's how it is
isn't it
with insurance
you always forget to protect yourself against
SOMETHING

and then luke is alone
and then the tiger growls
and then the tiger stalks towards luke
the tiger is limber and beautiful in its haute couture
it circles around luke
it licks its lips

the tiger
you tied the noose around your own neck

she picks up things that matter to him
things that make him who he is

the tiger
your first baby picture

she tears it up and throws it out

the tiger
your favorite blanket

out the window

the tiger
a scrapbook you made for me in first grade

out

the tiger
your house keys

out

the tiger
you favorite book

out

the tiger
i will erase you
and you will no longer exist to me
no longer my son

luke
please don't say that

the tiger
you did this

luke
im sorry

she picks up the joy division record
luke
no
pleaseplease

the tiger
first love
oh this is precious to you isn't it

luke
please
                    she SNAPS it in half
                        he slides down into the corner

        from another part of the stage
                            vivienne watches
                and then
                    just when the tiger goes to eat luke
vivienne
mother don't

the tiger
ive been waiting for you

vivienne
well im here now

the tiger
do mommy a favor and play her her favorite song wont you

vivienne
mother

the tiger
right over there

vivienne
but

the tiger
NOW
                    the tiger throws a glare and a growl her way
                            it frightens her
                vivienne walks over to the violin and begins to play
the tiger
now that's a good girl
                    the violin plays

the tiger stalks over to luke
            she gets closer and closer to him
      until he can feel her breath on his skin

the tiger
what a disappointment you turned out to be
stupid modern american boy
shameless impulsive failure
thats who you are
                  vivienne stops playing the violin
vivienne
that's enough
what about you

the tiger
what about me

vivienne
youre a failure
                  a deep growl
the tiger
what did you say

vivienne
we could have gotten straight a's
and perfect jobs
the house
and the lawn
the prizes you so adore

the tiger
i wanted people to respect me
to respect you
to respect us

vivienne
i got into harvard mother
but i decided not to go

the tiger
and now youll suffer for it

vivienne
no mother
youre going to suffer
you are
because you failed mother
mother

mother
mother
mother
you FAILED
you don't even have our respect

the tiger
when im done with him
youll be next
        the tiger makes a giant growl
    like its about to tear luke to pieces
       and then with all her might
       vivienne runs up to the tiger
  and smashes the violin over her head
         darkness
  the sounds of the violin being smashed over and over
         and over and over
            and over and over
      as this happens a fucked up menacing violin song plays
            it reverberates
      it stretches like its being ripped apart
  the rest of the cast appears
      they do their fucked up gesture dance to the violent sounds
         everything being ripped apart
    chaos
      and frenzy
         they are trying to keep up
 but its all too much
    its all too quick
      and they can barel keep up
   pushing themselves further and further and further
      pushing themselves almost out of their bodies
   trying to push themselves forward
 trying to keep up
      blackout

END OF ACT TWO.

act three

scene.

> *ten years later*
> *the sounds of a street in Brooklyn*
> *kaelan stands in a suit and tie on a tree lined street*
> *he checks his watch*
> *he takes a seat on a bench looking around*
> *waiting*
> *after a moment he looks at his watch again and paces*
> *he pulls out his cell phone and makes a call*

kaelan
hey
its kaelan
its two forty five
your fifteen minutes late
our appointment is at three
i told you
i need everything to run smoothly today
text me as soon as you get here
hop in a cab
just get here
okay

> *he hangs up the phone*
> *and looks at his watch again*
> *after a minute*
> *luke casually takes a seat next to him*
> *they don't recognize each other*
> *and then luke checks out kaelan*
> *and makes the connection*

luke
kaelan

kaelan
yes

> *a moment where they both awkwardly look at each other*

kaelan
luke

luke
hey!
hey
HEY

> *they hug*

kaelan
what are you –

luke
waiting to pick up-

kaelan
you have a kid here

luke
oh no no
not me no
never-

kaelan
no-

luke
a friend
im picking up my friends daughter

kaelan
oh-

luke
yea-

kaelan
oh-

luke
wait do you-

kaelan
no-

luke
no-

kaelan
sort of-

luke
sory of-

kaelan
well we're here for an interview

luke
we

kaelan
my son and i

luke
hes-

kaelan
late
i mean
his nanny
shes supposed to meet me here
i was at work
we have a
a you know
an interview thing
at three
so that's why im
yea
you look great

luke
thanks
you too yea
so you have a son

kaelan
yea

luke
wow

kaelan
i know

luke
how old is he

kaelan
four

luke
four
wow
that's
wow
that's amazing

that's
you know
so adult of you

kaelan
i know right
it's a
yea
i never thought i was the type
but yea
i guess i am

luke
definitely
definitely
i bet youre a great father

kaelan
do you

luke
you were always so
open

kaelan
right
thanks

luke
nurturing

kaelan
that sweet

luke
and youre in a suit

kaelan
yea

luke
and tie

kaelan
i know

luke

youre a-

kaelan
doctor

luke
wow

kaelan
its
you know
busy
and you

luke
i
me

kaelan
yea

luke
i work in marketing

kaelan
marketing

luke
you know
that's the
vague
the vague
im a graphic designer

kaelan
right brain

luke
no surprise there

kaelan
yea well
its all the same

luke
so youre married

kaelan
separated

luke
oh okay
sorry to hear that

kaelan
no
its
for the better

luke
yea

kaelan
yea
and you

luke
single
single
single
perpetually single

kaelan
i don't believe it

luke
im emotionally damaged
that's what i tell people

kaelan
so youre normal

luke
i have commitment issues

a phone rings
the ring tone is "love will tear us apart"

kaelan
im sorry
i have to take this

luke
yea sure

kaelan

how far are you guys
okay
fine
yea
that's fine
its okay
                    he hangs up the phone
luke
everything okay

kaelan
yea
                    luke is smiling
kaelan
what
          luke sings a piece of the old joy division song
                    kaelan laughs
                         its lovely
kaelan
still my favorite band
                    a moment
               and then
                         the moment
                    is broken
          as kaelan checks his watch
luke
you look stressed

kaelan
yea
its like a fuckin war zone getting kids into a good school these days
they want to interview them
have them play with crayons and look at pictures
want to make sure their parents are well mannered
and well dressed and well heeled
and that the kids are taken care of and will grow up to be senators and cure
diseases
you know because they can tell all of this from like age two
when theyre crawling around
in like diapers and stuff
its just

luke
you don't have to send him to a place like this

kaelan
public school

are you kidding me
yea right
then he'll end up at the bottom percentage
for like
for like
life you know
no
i cant have that
i have to give him all the things my parents didn't give me
things are going to be different with him
ill be different
that's important to me

luke
hey
you turned out pretty okay
and those cheek bones
they gave you a good jaw line

kaelan
thanks
i just want to be good for him you know

luke
you are

kaelan
you don't know that

luke
you wouldn't be here if you weren't
                              a moment
kaelan
its really good to see you

luke
thanks
you too
do you live nearby

kaelan
harlem

luke
uptown
fancy
nice

163

kaelan
where are you

luke
staten island

kaelan
oh
the island
i hear it's a good investment
more room

luke
i like it
so

kaelan
so

luke
do you
do you maybe want to go out sometime

kaelan
like to lunch

luke
like on a date

kaelan
oh
i don't
i don't know

luke
yea totally
no big deal
i get it

kaelan
its not you
its just that
with my son
and work

luke
i understand

kaelan
it just seems like our lives are-

luke
right

kaelan
and when im not at the hospital working all those hours
i have to spend every minute of my time with him
you know
they don't stay young forever

luke
yea

kaelan
there never seems to be enough time
it just
it flies
man does it fly

luke
id really love to meet him

kaelan
definitely

luke
hey

kaelan
hey

luke
we're adults

kaelan
doesn't feel like it

luke
tell me about it
                a breath
luke
do you think its fate

us seeing each other here
like we're tethered together or something

kaelan
you just said that
you really believe in stuff like that

luke
these days
i don't know what i believe anymore

a moment
kaelan
here they come
walking up
right there

luke
where

kaelan
that's my boy
that's my boy
that's my boy

and they wave
smiling

scene.

the waiting room of a private clinic
it is mostly calm and quiet
except for the sound of the television in the background
maybe a baby crying
the sound of an elevator
vivienne sits waiting
she stares out into nothingness
and then the sound of a phone ringing
she pulls it out
about to answer
looks at whos calling with a perplexed look on her face
and then silences it
after a moment
the elevator opens and a handsome man in his thirties
comes out
he seems rushed, disheveled

jack
vivienne
thank god youre here
i came as soon as i got your message

vivienne
i didn't mean to disrupt your day
its not a big deal

jack
of course it is

vivienne
im not scared

jack
i know youre not scared

vivienne
then

jack
youre so calm

vivienne
im sorry i alarmed you

jack
i just

vivienne
what

jack
i know youre not the most emotional person

vivienne
whats that supposed to mean

jack
you should be feeling things

vivienne
i am feeling things
don't tell me what im feeling
fuck do you think i am

jack
im your boyfriend

vivienne
not my father
see the distinction

jack
blow me

vivienne
watch it

jack
im sorry
im freaking out

vivienne
clearly
>   *the phone rings*
>   *she looks at her phone again*
>   *confused look on her face*

jack
what is it

vivienne
its my brother

jack
i thought you guys didn't really-

vivienne
me too
                              she silences the phone
jack
don't you think we should talk about this

vivienne
i wasn't feeling well
i got checked out
now im taking care of it

jack
i walk out of my meeting
look at my cellphone
missed call from my girlfriend
my girlfriend
who i happen to love very much
check your message
the words kept getting jumbled up in my head
they kept turning into static as you said them
i had to keep playing the message over and over and over
you know how many times i played it

vivienne
how many

jack
fourteen

vivienne
wow

jack
i had to play the message fourteen times just to understand what you were saying
now i may not be the most intellectually savvy person
but im not a total fuckin idiot
so
you can imagine
how hard it must have been to hear that

vivienne
oh was it
hard to hear that
because im the one who had to say it jack
me
im the one who said those words

not you
me
me
me

jack
ok
i get it

vivienne
do you
me
because i said it

jack
i got it

vivienne
good

jack
so what do we do

vivienne
we don't do anything

jack
so what do you do

vivienne
im doing it

jack
don't i have a say in this

vivienne
don't turn this into a fucking lifetime movie

jack
fuck off
im here
im not trying to make this harder

vivienne
then don't

jack
i just
i think we should talk about it

vivienne
we have
before

jack
that was then
this is now

vivienne
i don't want to have kids
it wasn't a secret the day you met me
it wasn't a secret on our first date or after our first kiss
it wasn't a secret the first time we slept together or when we decided to move in
together
it was a conversation we had clearly
it was a conversation i was clear about
and one that you agreed on
i said i don't want to have kids
i cant
and you said okay
fine
i understand
i agree
i don't need them
that's fine
that's what you said
not once
or twice
but multiple times

jack
i thought

vivienne
what did you think

jack
people change
all the time
their thoughts
their opinions
they evolve
they digresss

i thought when this moment happened
any number of possibilities
could take shape
could manipulate the air around us
could turn you around

vivienne
this wasn't planned
or on purpose
it was something that happened
and now its going to be something thatll unhappen
and things can stay the same
its that simple

jack
its not that simple

vivienne
it is
IT IS

jack
you think im going to look at you the same

vivienne
what

jack
you think ill hear your voice the same way
that the image i have of you from last night and this morning and right now
will stay the same
it cant

vivienne
youre not the only one that can change things in his head jack

jack
just consider

vivienne
there is nothing to consider
you may be weak

jack
weak

vivienne
you may be weak but i am not
i know what i want
i cant
i wont

jack
please
just go home with me tonight

vivienne
i cant

jack
if you don't want to have it tomorrow
ill come back with you
ill be supportive
just go home
sleep on it

vivienne
no

jack
why not

vivienne
because i wouldn't be a good mother

jack
you don't know that

vivienne
because a child needs more emotion and attention than i am capable of giving

jack
false

vivienne
because we don't have enough space in our apartment

jack
we'll move

vivienne
because i cant stay at home and take care of the baby

jack
i will

vivienne
oh you will

jack
yes
besides these are all just stupid shitty excuses that any person can throw out
any person
who is
who is

vivienne
who is what

jack
acting like a coward
                    silence
                            silence
                                    silence
jack
i love you
but youre acting like a coward
                            silence
vivienne
because we cant afford it

jack
ill get another job

vivienne
doing what
serving at a bar catering
as someones assistant
what are you qualified to do
maybe you can come into my office
and be my assistant
take down my coffee orders
thatll pay the bills

jack
ouch
ouch
fuck you
that was really

vivienne
it's the truth

jack
i have a job

vivienne
designing sets
isn't exactly bringing in the health insurance and the big paycheck now is it

jack
i didn't know you had a problem with my job

vivienne
i don't

jack
it sure sounds like you do

vivienne
if it makes you happy
its what makes me happy
so im happy for you

jack
bullshit

vivienne
i love your job
i love that youre an artist and do what you want
i love that
but its not enough
for this
for a baby
for a family
its not enough

jack
youre miserable aren't you

vivienne
excuse me

jack
i did what i wanted with my life
and you resent me for that
that unlike you

i didn't take some shitty job

vivienne
that shitty job pays for everything you have

jack
im sorry that you wanted to be a photographer and you didn't do it
im sorry that you didn't have the balls to do what you want in this life

vivienne
fuck you
you don't know a thing
you don't know what it means to be an adult
to make sacrifices
youre just some silly overgrown child
trying to play adult
you know nothing
silence
                    silence
jack
if im not good enough
why are you with me

vivienne
i wish i could do this without hurting you
but i cant

jack
you could have picked anybody else

vivienne
i picked you

jack
and what if i want to have a baby

vivienne
then youre with the wrong person

jack
how do you know that

vivienne
because ive already made up my mind

jack
i don't believe you

vivienne
when someone tells you who they are
or what they want
you should believe them

jack
i love you

> she looks at him
> > she looks at him
> and starts to cry
> > she doesn't wail or scream or moan or have a break down
> its very soft
> its very held back
> > a moment
> > > and then
> > the sound of a text on a phone
> vivienne looks at it

vivienne
WHAT DO YOU WANT

> and then everything SHATTERS

jack
what is it
what does it say

vivienne
its my mother
i have to go

jack
wait

vivienne
i cant do this right now

jack
when someone tells you-

> and then
> > that terrible overwhelming static noise
> as jack becomes
> the old fashioned traveling salesman

jack/traveling salesman
you should believe them

> blackout

scene.
vivienne wears all black
there is a giant beautiful tree near her
she is wearing shades and her arms are crossed
after a moment
derek enters

derek
you look beautiful

vivienne
what are you doing here

derek
came to pay my respects

vivienne
thank you

derek
im sorry for your loss

vivienne
really

derek
that's what youre supposed to say isn't it
that's the tradition

vivienne
traditions are stupid

derek
not all of them

vivienne
you always were old fashioned
always did what mom and dad wanted you to do

derek
they've set me off on the right path

vivienne
hows california

derek
ive been back for a while now
in the old neighborhood

a block from my parents
they need me you know
its important to be close to family

vivienne
look at you

derek
im an engineer now

vivienne
of course you are

derek
what about you

vivienne
i moved to chicago

derek
chicago
really

vivienne
i wanted to get lost somewhere
reinvent myself

derek
and did you

vivienne
no

derek
what do you do

vivienne
youll never guess

derek
youre a lawyer

vivienne
me
a lawyer

derek
you were always strong
had some fight in you

vivienne
im a photographer

derek
well look at you
a grown up photographer

vivienne
i didn't say grown up
it's a good hobby though

derek
so then what

vivienne
im a professor of mathematics

derek
and are you happy viv
                              a moment
vivienne
are you
                    a moment
                        and then
              they hug awkwardly
derek
well its good to see you

vivienne
you too derek
              and then he goes
                        she stands there in silence for a moment
          and then
                  luke arrives
luke
staying long

vivienne
no
im going back tomorrow

luke
quick trip

vivienne
only came to bury mother
say good bye one last time

luke
i cant believe she killed herself

vivienne
dramatic till the end

luke
she would do that
she would kill herself

vivienne
she did

                        a moment

vivienne
what aren't you telling me

luke
nothing

              a moment

luke
she was sick

vivienne
sick
sick how

luke
she had cancer

vivienne
what kind

luke
does it matter
the bad kind

vivienne
i didn't know

luke
of course you didn't

vivienne
whats the supposed to mean

luke
she didn't want you to know vivienne
i don't even know why she told me

vivienne
so she killed herself
didn't want anyone to see her deteriorate from the beautiful
perfect thing that she was
makes sense

luke
youre wrong you know

vivienne
then why

luke
because we abandoned her viv
because she had no one left
because unlike the other chinese families that she knew
her kids weren't around to make sure she didn't die alone
the shame in that

vivienne
in the end its always about shame
well i didn't know

luke
would it have changed anything
                                            silence
luke
she died alone viv
alone
the worst kind of death
don't worry
i wasn't here either

vivienne
so that's it huh
a whole life lived
                                      silence
              silence
                                silence
vivienne

i miss dad
a moment

luke
kaelan came
he has this whole other life
what if
what if
this is all there is
its just who we are
what if its just in our character
what if this is who you are
and who i am
and who he is
what if theres no changing things
what if its too late
and ive already missed out on
what if no one ever looks at me
what if that's not even the point
to be something to someone
to be anything
what if the things we want will never fit together

vivienne
youre asking the wrong person

> *silence as they look at the old neighborhood*
> *the sounds in the distance*
> *of laughing children*
> *of the wind blowing*
> *of family*
> *of life*
> *the old one*
> *the one that never changes*

luke
so

vivienne
so

luke
whats new
anything new with you

vivienne
yea
yea there is

luke
what

> they stand in silence
> we hear the birds
> and the trees rustling
> and the wind
> the wind picks up
> and it blows some leaves
> ... the leaves and the wind
> and the wind
> and the wind
> until the leaves are everywhere
> so many leaves
> so many leaves everywhere
> and the wind
> so much wind
> until they are just covered...
> and disappear
> blackout

END OF ACT TWO

epilogue

scene.

> *the future*
>> *luke wears a suit and tie*
>> *he sits in a beautiful office with floor to ceiling windows*
> *the views outside the window are stunning*
>> *they are really high up*
> *its not new york*
>> *its not even america*
>>> *we're in china now*
>>> *sonya washington sits in front of luke*
>> *she is a powerful woman*
>>> *in a powerful suit*
>>>> *in a powerful position*
>>>>> *in a powerful company*

sonya
youre fluent in four languages

luke
english
spanish
i can speak cantonese AND mandarin
and i also know some french and german

sonya
impressive

luke
i also know some ASL

sonya
your degrees and your grades speak for themselves

luke
thank you

sonya
and you really want to be here
in china

luke
it's a beautiful place
and my family
this is where they came from
so im home in a sense
and this company

sonya
this company

luke
is at the forefront of the global market
what you do here

sonya
is ahead of the game

luke
its remarkable
theres nowhere else id rather be
a hundred percent
i am committed to being a part of this company and being the best employee
possible
i will work tirelessly for you
my skills-

sonya
speak for themselves

luke
i think youll find that ill be an excellent addition to this corporation

sonya
to this monolith

there is a knock at the door

sonya
one moment please

luke
absolutely

sonya
come in

william grant enters the office
he is very familiar
a tinge of purple

william
i have that information you asked about

sonya
and

william
well

he puts a file on her desk
and then whispers in her ear
a sharp static fills the air
as he whispers he points at different things in the files
different pages
her face becomes dismayed

sonya
mister Andrews

luke
Anthony
please call me Anthony

sonya
mister anthony andrews
this is my collague

luke
its nice to meet you

a look

luke
you look familiar
have we met before

a look

luke
at one of my previous interviews here maybe

william
highly unlikely
i just started working here
i used to work in insurance
back when it meant something

sonya
not anymore

william
not anymore

luke
i don't think i caught your name

sonya
hes one of our in house research specialists

luke
oh
interesting
what kind of research do you do

william
people research
you for instance

luke
me
sure
like where i went to school
and my grades and such

william
it's a little bit more personal im afraid

sonya
my colleague has brought me some interesting
finds
we'll call them finds about you
finds that
honestly

luke
finds
what finds

sonya
well for one
mister anthony andrews
it says here your given name is luke wood

luke
it was
my name was luke wood
but i changed it a long time ago
everything in those files
my grades
languages
accomplishments
theye all mine
i just
i changed my name

sonya
why

luke
it didn't fit

william
it didn't fit

sonya
that's interesting isn't it

william
it is
it didn't fit or you wanted to be someone else

luke
i wanted to start over
be better
be different

sonya
unfortunately
mister wood
mister luke wood
that's not possible
you cant just become someone else whenever you want
and so now that this new setback has presented itself

william
we have to review your file
together

sonya
my colleague has been a busy man
haven't you

william
i certainly have

sonya
and you've found some interesting things like this
looks like some kind of party
and there is
well

william
theres a lot of cocaine in that picture with you mister wood

luke
let me see that
                    she hands it to him
luke
that was a long time ago
at a college party
and it wasn't even mine
i didn't even know that picture existed

william
thats what im here for

sonya
he can find anything on the internet
anything on the server
anything on the ether about you

luke
this picture

sonya
could make the company look bad
irresponsible
if those are the types of people we are hiring
drug addicts

luke
im not a drug addict

sonya
what you do behind closed doors is your business

william
just don't get caught

luke
one picture

sonya
oh theres more

luke
more

william
this business with your sister
a
what did you call it
a dick sucking list

sonya
that is really inappropriate mister wood
makes me feel really uncomfortable when i have to hear those words

luke
i was a kid

sonya
kid or no kid mister wood

william
what you do is going to follow you forever

luke
i didn't know

sonya
the fact that you would do this
to your own family
it seems like you don't have any
whats the word im looking for

william
loyalty

sonya
exactly
how can we hire someone we cant even trust
so many precious secrets
so much information
at this corporation

william
this monolith

sonya
whoever works with us must be trusted

william
can you be trusted mister wood

luke
i can
i can

william
we'll see about that

sonya
we have a lot of files to go through

william
you've been a very very busy man mister wood

sonya
shut the door will you
this might take a while

the tiger appears
unseen to the characters
maybe as before
maybe broken and disheveled
now less powerful...
powerless?

the tiger
as the door slowly shuts
we watch for a brief moment as they begin to go over the files
luke sits in his chair
uncomfortable
sad
terrified
broken

luke
i just want it to go away
i just want it to go away

the tiger
but it doesn't
it never does
not anymore

blackout

END OF PLAY

what came after.

christopher oscar peña

what came after was commissioned by Pine Box Theater Company and produced as part of ElectionFest2012 at Theater Wit in Chicago, IL. Opening night was on October 23, 2012. The piece was directed by Lisa Portes and featured Karen Aldridge (mother/grandmother), Kristina Valada-Viars (daughter), and Gabi Mayorga (the kid).

Special thanks to Susan Bowen

this play is for all the mothers
          and especially my friend Jenna (Daniels) Nohel
    for all the faith

and for Kristen Connolly
          heart of hearts

characters

father/grandfather	*extremely conservative, republican, Christian type*
daughter	*scared, a lamb in a world of wolves*
the kid	*just that*

time

the recent past *if we're lucky*

the recent future *if we're not*

and somewhere else, maybe, today

a note on casting:

daughter should always be played by a woman... because you know, men cant have babies... yet

father/grandfather can be played by a woman (pronouns to be changed)

the kid can be either a guy or a girl.... adjusting the pronouns so that he/she is gay/lesbian

finally, though the natural impulse is to cast father/grandfather as a white male, real life isn't always this way is it? the character could be a black woman, a mixed races man, or anything in between. choices are good.

part one.

darkness
> *in the darkness terrifying sounds*
> *a mix of sounds that create a nightmarish landscape*
> *a girl laughs*
> *sounds of footsteps and running*
> *the sound of a subway car going by*
> *the alarm of a car going off*
> *the roar of a tiger*
> *heavy rain fall*
> *the sound of a dam breaking*

heavy breathing
> *crying*
> *another laugh*
> *an old nineties song that used to comfort you*
> *another laugh*
> *and then finally*

> *the real scream of a girls voice*
> *the girl is screaming in bed*
> *a door to her room opens and the lights come on*
> *her father is there*

father
wake up Katie
wake up
baby im here
it was only a nightmare
you were having a nightmare

> *she wakes up clutching to him*

im here now
im here now
it was only a nightmare
its not real

daughter
how can you say that
it is real
every thing about this is real

father
just breathe

daughter
I cant
daddy I cant live like this

father
it will get better
I promise
itll be in the past
ill take care of you

daughter
it wont
not until its out of me

father
what

daughter
I cant daddy I cant
I cant have this baby

father
Katie
think about what youre saying

daughter
as long as theres a child it wont be behind me
itll be right in front of me
every day
every single day of my life looking back at me
its eyes
its mouth
its voice
every thing a sharp memory shooting pieces of shrapnel at me

father
go back to sleep
every thing will be okay
                              he starts to go
daughter
I want to have an abortion

father
I am a patient god fearing man

daughter
how can you still say that
I was raped dad
I was raped
where was your god then

father
you've been through a lot
so ill forgive you for saying that this once

daughter
why

father
youre paying
we all pay
for our sins

daughter
this baby

father
is gods will
if the baby wasn't meant to be
your body would have stopped it
god wouldn't have let it

daughter
im going to do it dad
whether you like it or not

father
you're a minor
you wont do it
you cant
not without my consent
not without my money
with what Katie

daughter
don't you care about me

father
of course I do
as your father
every piece of me wants nothing more than to protect you
to do whats best
and like a parent
you should feel the same way
there is a baby inside of you
a baby that knows nothing of this world
who is not to blame

who is pure and innocent
god has given you a small innocent treasure to raise
you were chosen
and now its my job to protect it as much as I would protect you
we must protect the helpless
the voiceless
don't you see Katie
out of something terrible
you have the ability
the option
the choice
to do something good
love that baby
rise above it
this is your test

he starts to go

daughter
Abraham

father
what

daughter
you would sacrifice everything
you would sacrifice your child for the promise of something youre not even sure
is real

father
im doing the best I can

daughter
im going to do it

father
im sorry that you were under the impression that this was a discussion between
two adults
youre just a young woman
you don't know whats right for you
you don't know whats right
that's what im here for
one day youll thank me
one day youll thank me for making the right choice for you
one day youll thank me for knowing better

blackout

part two.

time passes
years later

the father is now an old man
time has not been kind to him
he sits with the kid, his grandchild

they sit at chick-fil-a

grandfather
hows your sandwich sport

the kid
delicious

grandfather
best sandwiches in town right

the kid
I could eat this every day
for breakfast
for lunch
for dinner
I could eat it between snacks too
chick-fil-a all day every day

grandfather
im glad to hear youre happy
you know your mom used to love chick-fil-a too

the kid
she did

grandfather
it was her favorite
we would come here every Wednesday night for dinner
I would offer to take her to really expensive nice fancy restaurants
but no
she wanted her chick-fil-a
it was her favorite
she would be happy to see us here together
like this
laughing
she would like to see you smile

a sound or light shift

the kid stands up and addresses the audience

the kid
not everything in life is terrible
often we try to look at things in black and white
so many of us think that its one way or the other
but the truth is
most of life is gray
most of life is complicated

she looks at grandfather

look at us
hes so happy
and me
the happiness I felt now
in that moment
before I knew about disease and politics
before I knew about heartbreak and misogyny
before someone turned their back on me
before I betrayed someone
before lies and heartache and scars and wounds
before I learned that not everything is fair
that we are not all the same
that we don't all get what we want
that you should always watch your back
that anything can strike
this moment
before I had beliefs
and those beliefs were tested and sometimes broken
before
before
before
the world
I was happy
I didn't know anything
and I miss this moment
I hold it in the back of my head
I hold it in the spot closest to my heart
I hold it on the freckle on the top of my left foot
I hold onto it
I hold onto him
even though what came after
even though what came after-
well

the kid goes back to sit down with grandfather

the kid
grandpa

grandfather
yes kiddo

the kid
youre the best

grandfather
thanks kiddo
youre the best too
and I love ya

the kid
grandpa
why are there so many people outside
they look angry
and they have all those signs

grandfather
well kiddo
there are some people
some very very bad deviant people who are mad at the chick-fil-a
they are mad the chick-fil-a supports Christians
and god
and the righteous
they are confused sick people
who need help
but they don't seek it out
instead they try to spread their disease and their poison around the world
they are trying to shut this place down

the kid
no

grandfather
yep
so we are here kiddo
we are here to support the chick-fil-a people
but more importantly
we are here for what we believe in

the kid
what do we believe in grandpa

grandfather

god
>
> *a breath*

the kid
you wont leave me too will you
you wont kill yourself the way mom did right

grandfather
no kiddo
never
its you and me
you and me forever okay

the kid
okay

grandfather
your mother loved you very much
she just
she just wasn't made for this world
but shes watching over you
you know that right
you know that

> *but the kid just stares into space*
> > *and the grandfather looks at the kid*
> > *the grandfathers words floating in space*
> *because sometimes*
> > *sometimes hes not sure he believes it either*

blackout

part three

the kid appears

the kid
do you think its possible to look at something
to hold it in your hand
and to feel utter happiness and utter pain at the same time
to hold that thing in your head
in your heart

there is a memory in my mind
a moment
it is both beautiful and excruciating

it is years later and I am in love
I have met someone
I have met the one
maybe
and she is
she laughs

we hear her laugh
and it soothes me
on our first date we share a strawberry milk shake
even though later on I find out she hates strawberries
I memorize the dots on her back
little moles that seem to form new and undiscovered constellations
she tells me about how when she was little
if she got sick
her mother would lay in bed with her all night and sing her the song fever

the voice of a girl sings fever
maybe the kid joins in
our first kiss is in wicker park
our second is on the beach
or what I thought was the beach
I take her on a date to the most beautiful place I know
she laughs and says
this aint no beach
she was a californian
she promises to one day show me the pacific ocean

it is beautiful
everything is beautiful
but we always have to hide
she doesn't like this

but she respects me
and we are careful
we are always careful

until one day
when we're at home kissing
and we don't hear the sound of the car pulling into the driveway
and the sound of his boots on the gravel
and the key turning the door knob
we don't hear any of this
because we are too deep in each other
fallen
down the rabbit hole

and then
he comes through the door and tears us apart
and I am
and I am
and I am
shocked
and I am
and I am
scared
and I am
and I am

the grandfather appears

grandfather
disgusting

the kid
and I am
and I am

grandfather
sinful and ungodly

the kid
and I am
and I am
and I am

grandfather
not my blood
not my progeny
not my family

the kid
and I am
and I am
and I am

grandfather
dead to me

the kid
and this moment replays in my head
my whole life
over and over and over
the way it feels to touch her skin
the way it feels to kiss her
the way it feels to be
to be to be
and I am
and I am

grandfather
dead to me

the kid
and this moment replays in my head
my whole life
over and over and over
the way it feels to lose a father
the way it feels to lose a name
the way it feels to be alone
the way it feels to be
to be to be
and I am

grandfather
dead to me

the kid
this one moment
this one moment of true bliss
and sheer horror
this one moment
I cant seem to let go of

grandfather
I wish youd never been born
I wish your mother had aborted you
you are dead to me

the kid
and I am
and I am
and I am
alone

the grandfather vanishes
and then a flicker of light
bright bright bright bright light
and daughter/mother appears

mother
dear baby
I wanted to tell you
that you are meant for greatness
that you will have a fire in you that will spark the world
I wanted to tell you
that I am not strong enough
some of us are chosen
you are
I wanted to tell you that no matter what it seems like
I was scared of not being courageous enough for you
because you are pure
and nothing is your fault
I wanted to tell you that I was scared of being your mother
afraid to look at you and not be enough
I wanted to tell you
something
for which words will never be enough
but most importantly
I wanted to tell you
that I love
that I love you
but most importantly

the kid
and I am
and I am
and I am

mother
I wanted to tell you
that you are not alone

the kid
and I am
and I am

and I am

mother
not alone
you are not alone

the kid
and I am
and I am
and I am

blackout

end of play

snow storm

christopher oscar peña

snow storm was produced as part of Rattlestick Playwrights Theater's (David Van Asselt, Artistic Director) **theaterjam3** on Sunday, March 11th, 2012. The play was directed by Mary Birnbaum and featured Condola Rashad (laura), Randy Harrison (ben), and Mikaela Feely-Lehmann (stacey).

special thanks: Daniel Tallbot, Eugenia Furneaux, Molly Ward, and Rodney To.

FOR
>*my boys on sueño:*
>>*david terra*
>*derek noone*
>>>*john kincheloe*
>>*kit ko*
>>>*hassan elhaj*
>>*danh huynh*
>>>>*and dustin cathcart*

for all the secrets

>*and to maya herr-anderson*

for all the same reasons

characters

laura
stacey
ben

setting

now, a bedroom in the city

in the darkness we hear sounds
            HOT sounds
                sounds with sweat and lots and lots of moisture
you totally want to know what they are
actually
        you really just want to be there
and then
                        we can see EVERYTHING
        a guy
            and two girls
                    yes TWO
        NAKED
            and around them
                    mountains
                    and
            mountains
                    and MOUNTAINS
                        of snow
        not that kind
                THAT KIND

laura
oh my god my jaw aches

stacey
mine too

laura
what the fuck is wrong with you?

ben
im sorry!

laura
not as sorry as i am

stacey
i suddenly don't feel very pretty
why do i suddenly feel like im in high school again

laura
WOULD YOU STOP GRINDING YOUR FUCKIN TEETH!

ben
i cant control it!

laura
youre lucky you don't have to blow yourself
chew youre own dick off

ben
lets just give it a few minutes

laura
does this happen to you often?

ben
NO
NEVER Tell her babe

stacey
NEVER
hes always hard!
we have sex!
TONS AND TONS of HOT-
maybe youre just nervous
that's it right?
YOURE JUST NERVOUS!
i mean two hot women-

laura
two VERY hot women

stacey
the hottest women you know
that's totally it

> laura *pulls out a giant PINK vibrator*
> *it probably makes you nervous*
> *or excited*
> *depends on what kind of person you are*
> *no judgement*

ben
jesus!
would you put that thing away
its PINK FOR GODS SAKE

laura
if youre not gonna do the work
SOMETHING HAS TO DO IT!
> *she turns it on*
> *its LOUD*
> *like horror movie*

CHAIN SAW LOUD

ben
HOLY!
fuck that
does that thing have its own charger you know over night
do you plug it in?
fuck!
GET THAT THING AWAY FROM ME!

laura
don't be such a fuckin vagina

stacey
we just need music
you know
maybe we've set the wrong mood
the ambiance
maybe its just not right

ben
good idea
good THINKING

> stacey *gets up and plugs in an ipod*
> *the first thing that comes on is berlins "take my breath away"*
> laura *tenses up*
> *all the muscles on her face*
> *they get so tight it hurts*

laura
are you serious?
i cant believe you own this fuckin song
i danced with drew duncan to this song at high school prom
he had two left feet

ben
that guy was a fucktard

laura
what did you call him?

ben
you heard me

laura
a fucktard
who the fuck is a fucktard
WHO CALLS SOMEBODY A FUCKTARD

you you you

stacey
guys-

ben
me WHAT?

laura
you FUCKIN BITCHHEAD

ben
good one

stacey
you guys
maybe this is a sign
i think
this is maybe karma's way of saying

ben
WHAT

stacey
i don't know
maybe we're not supposed to be doing this
maybe im not sure
im not sure im so comfortable anymore

laura
fuckin great

ben
no no NO!
you cant back out now
its my birthday
you said this was my birthday present
you cant give someone a fuckin present
and then i don't know
take it back
that's just
that's just RUDE
plain rude

laura
hes right you know

stacey
okay maybe i just need a few minutes to collect myself
is that the right phrase?
collect myself?
did you guys know that people call doing blow skiing?
isn't that funny?
i JUST heard that for the first time at work
like apparently that terms been around since the eighties
AND I JUST DIDN'T KNOW
i mean people say they say
they say stuff like
do you have any snow?
so of course like obviously
OBVIOUSLY
it would make sense to "go skiing"
but i just didn't get that
i just figured it out
a bit slow i guess
skiing
skiing
did you guys knows that sonny bono died because he was skiing
he like crashed into a tree
horrible accident WHAT a way to go
like your body exploding
just like blood
tons and tons of blood everywhere
just splattered all over this blanket OF
of white white snow
like a jackson pollock
maybe it wasn't a horrific accident
maybe he was skiing and he thought to himself
my life is awful
im just going to crash into this tree
i thought this is what you wanted
i thought you wanted this
i thought this would make you HAPPY

ben
it does
it DOES
baby this is all ive been thinking about

stacey
THEN WHY ARENT YOU FUCKIN HARD?!
i need some blow
laura PASS ME THE FUCKIN BLOW
don't horde it

> laura *does a line*
> *a big one*
> *she likes them big*
> *more than she can handle*
> *but she would never admit that*

laura
fuck
FUCK
it burns!
that one fuckin BURNED!

ben
fuck fuck fuck
work
get hard
why wont you fuckin work
maybe its not me
its not me
FUCK IT
its not me
maybe we should
i don't know
lets watch jeopardy or something
for a little while

laura
does it look like im here to FUCKIN WATCH JEOPARDY?

stacey
ive never seen a vibrator that big

laura
really?
didn't you like have one?
like growing up

stacey
i didn't
i didn't really do that
my parents were like really moral
no bad words
and no R rated movies
and you know
saying grace at the table
and and and
like they didn't drink

i didn't drink until after college
and like i couldn't have sex
you know
i wasn't really raised THAT way

laura
WHAT WAY?

stacey
i just said
THAT way-

laura
what?
like im some slut
like im some fuckin kinda slut
THAT WAY?!
cuz im not sure if you looked around yet
but we've ended up in the same bed
the same EXACT BED at the same EXACT TIME
so whatever way
you THINK you are
youre NOT

stacey
that's not true
bens the only guys ive been with

laura
a lot of good that's doing you

ben
whats THAT supposed to mean?

laura
it means your DICK SUCKS
it means your dick is pathetic and small and useless
it means your dick is
not
even
useful
you don't even
FUNCTION
i thought drug dick was a myth
a SAD one
YOURE SO FUCKIN FRUSTRATING!

ben
ARE YOU TRYING TO HURT ME?!
why are you such a fuckin bitch all of a sudden
i would NEVER NEVER EVER
hurt you like that
i wouldn't
NO
because
you know ive
ive wanted to be with you
to feel what that was like
to feel what it must be like to be inside of you
to be part of you
since since
since we were
i don't know
sixteen or some shit
that's what ive wanted
i used to jerk off to you
two three times a day
like everywhere
you laura
YOU
you know
and then at some point
AT SOME FUCKIN POINT
in my own small
TOTALLY FUCKED UP
AH!
TOTALLY FUCKED UP
small
so small world
i realized how FUCKIN IN LOVE WITH YOU I WAS
so you know what
you know
i stopped jerking off to you
COMPLETELY
JUST STOPPED
because i didn't want to taint you
because i didn't want to make you dirty
because i just needed
because i JUST WANTED
i don't know
SO DON'T FUCKIN TALK TO ME LIKE THAT YOU DUMB BITCH

stacey
don't call her a bitch

ben
what?

stacey
you don't call someone you love a bitch

laura
you love me?

ben
YES

stacey
i think maybe this was a bad idea i think maybe i should go

ben
what?
no

laura
shut up and do a line

stacey
things are so painfully clear now
i need to stop skiing

ben
what?
no

stacey
i thought i would do this to make you happy
i thought i would do this because i loved you
but you don't love me
if i stop now maybe i can still take control of the situation
if i stop now
if i stop-

ben
its too late
youre totally fucked

stacey
apparently not
apparently your dick doesn't work
and somehow you've still managed to fuck me

OVER
> *she doesn't know why but shes leaving*
> *whatever she needs*
> *its not here*
> *shes gone*

laura
did you reall mean that?
did you really mean what you said?

ben
YES
yes
every word
> *she gets in really close to him*
> *its really*
> *really*
> *really*
> *fuckin*
> *sweet*

laura
youre starting to get hard

ben
see
maybe its just you i really wanted

laura
i remember drew duncan asked me to prom
and even though he had two left feet
i had the best time of my life
i used to wish it was you that i was dancing with
but you didn't ask me to prom
you didn't think i was pretty enough
the only thing i regret now
is not being there for duncan
not being there with him
not being totally in the moment
but im in the moment now
im in the moment with you
everythings so clear
and you wanna know a secret

ben
anything
> *she gets really close to his ear*
> *and then*
> *BITES IT*

HARD
        so painfully hard
                a little chunk comes off in her mouth
        she spits it out at him
laura
YOURE FUCKIN PATHETIC

        she gets up to leave
                hes screaming in agony
                        clutching his ear
        she throws the vibrator at him
                berlins "take my breath away" swells loud

        blackout

                                end of play.

however long the night

christopher oscar peña

however long the night was commissioned by the Old Vic/ New Voices and produced as part of the 2011 t.s. eliot US/UK Exchange at the Old Vic Theatre (Kevin Spacey, Artistic Director) in London on Friday, June 3, 2011. The piece was produced by Frances Black and directed by Mary Birnbaum. The cast featured Michael Bradley Cohen (brad), Michael Micalizzi (kel), Lourdes Aguilar (L), and Dominic Spillane (spill).

Special thank to Steve Stout, Janine Nabers, Jon Caren, Josh Conkel, Stephanie Ybarra, Mike Donahue, Roberta Pereira, Ella Hickson, and Oliver Rose.

For *dan barlow, tiffany rose brown, and michael boxall*
       and for zabie (elizabeth wueste) and freedo (wilfred torres)

for all the years

the backyard of a middle class house in the suburbs
  kel, late twenties, sits on a bench or a tree stump, bourbon in hand
    or maybe
      he just stands, staring up into the stars
    he wears a rumpled tuxedo, no jacket

  on another part of the stage
    brad *seems to float in mid air*

brad
there is a history on me
there is a history on all of us
that we can no longer control
we used to be made of organic particles
skin and fiber
blood and dust
but now theres chemical particles
mechanical particles
science and history particles
it marks every part of who we are
  after a moment
    L *walks in*
      she's wearing a fab dress

L
ive been looking for you everywhere

kel
you changed out of your wedding dress

L
was afraid some drunk asshole would accidentally spill something on it

kel
theres always that bitch at the party

L
why are you hiding out in the back yard

kel
just wanted to look out at the stars
remember when you shot me with a dart
it literally landed between my eyes

L
who steps in front of a dart board and yells BOO when people are playing darts?!

kel
we sat under this tree named the kids we didn't even have yet

L
oliver for you
brad for me

kel
lots of memories in this back yard

L
yes
now will you come back in please
you've been hiding out all night
hardly spoken a word to anyone
sour look on your face

kel
jetlag

L
youre my best friend
you have to entertain
its like your duty or something

kel
im not a monkey
there isn't a song and dance

L
kel youre not being very celebratory

kel
i came didn't i
im here

L
people are asking about you

kel
people
what people
who is asking about me
i hardly know most of those people

L
what are you talking about
we all went to school together

kel
that was another lifetime

L
you never told me what you thought

kel
about what

L
max

kel
what about him

L
us getting married
our relationship

kel
what does it matter
you married him didn't you
what do you care what i think
known him as long as you've known me

> spill *stumbles*
> > *into*
> > *the*
> > *backyard*
> > > *he is very handsome*
> > > *he no longer wears a button up*
> > > *just a white wife beater (how inappropriate)*
> > > > *did he just pee outside? –*
> > > *cuz he might be zipping up his fly*

spill
fuckin A man
what a great fuckin party

brad
my world ended before i ever had a chance for it to start
it was my fathers fault
and my fathers father
and his fathers father
and everyone that came before it

father
father

asshole
you told me you were a good person
you tried to shield me from the server
you told me never to ask about the server
to stay as far away from it as possible
you told me the server was bad
that you were protecting me from it
but the only thing you were protecting was yourself

you were gone by the time i looked into the server
gone before i could hate you in life
you knew eventually i would find out
you just made sure you were gone before you had to deal with the consequences

kel
great fuckin party
hey man im kel

L
spill you know my best friend kel
kel you've met spill before
he was maxs best man

kel
nice to meet you

spill
we've met

kel
i don't think we have

spill
we went to elementary school together
different high schools but were in school together all the way till eighth grade

kel
no i don't think so

spill
spill
dude
damien spillman

kel
sorry

spill
okay
you really don't remember me

L
he doesn't remember a lot of things

spill
come on man
you have to remember
i remember every detail of that time
i played baseball
shortstop
we won every game
my hair used to be lighter
we sat next to each other in mister reeds class in third grade
you read a lot
i remember you had these thick thick thick glasses
and you knew all the answers
but you were quiet a lot
i was the class clown
always had a joke
remember this one
whats green and smells like pork?
think about it
green and smells like pork?
nope
don't have it
kermit the frogs finger
AH!
that's a good one right

L
disgusting
and yet
amazing

kel
i remember growing up on sugarplum drive
how it took me years to figure out that all the streets in our neighborhood
were named after sweets
lollipop way
gumdrop avenue
i remember the sound of the pacific ocean
a constant symphony
and the thick feeling of cool moisture on my face
the taste of salt

making me feel like my particles were connected to the water
that i was the ocean
i remember the sound of my bedroom door always shaking
because i always slept with the window open
and it would create this sort of wind tunnel in my room
i remember my father waking me up every morning with a kiss on the cheek
and my mother driving me to school every day
my dog on my lap
that's what i remember when i think of this place

spill
yea
we got different memories i guess

kel
it would appear so

L
the great thing is
we're not stuck in the past
so theres always room for new ones
new memories i mean
kel and i are best friends and you and max are best friends
so we can all hang out
when you visit
we've been hanging out a lot kel
spill, max and i
and now that max and i are married
we'll be like a family
i miss you kel
i wish you hadn't moves so far away
i wish youd answer your phone more often

kel
i live in this building
twenty nine stories high
at the sourthern most tip of the island of manhattan
surrounded on all sides by water
sweeping endless views
a bridge here
a giant hole where huge towers once were
majestic
lights in buildings like stars
not like these stars
beautiful
but it might as well be a cave
no cell phone service in my apartment

stupid huh

L
maybe we can all come visit this year

spill
yea mean
that would be awesome
you can show us the town
ive never been there

kel
maybe

spill
man
being here with all these people
makes me wish we were young again
makes me wish we were all back in school
time of my life
best time of my life
it used to be so awesome
and now we're adults
with bills and shit
jobs
responsibilities
not like before
everything was so easy then
a simpler time when we were all just friends
no worries
aren't you guys nostalgic like i am

L
i am
all the time

kel
for what

spill
childhood-

kel
for what L
what are you nostalgic for

L

you know
when we were kids
everything was so nice
and simple

kel
are you out of your mind

L
what

kel
are you out of your fuckin mind
who are you

spill
chill bro

kel
im not your bro
im not your fuckin bro
you were fat L
when we were younger
you were enormous
people put twinkies in your locker
they made oinking noises when you walked by
OINK
OINK
OINK OINK
they called you miss piggy you idiot
yea i remember that joke spill
whats green and smells like pork
kermit the frogs finger after he'd gotten done with L
miss piggy
OINK OINK
OINK
did you forget that part of the joke
the punchline
because i didn't
i didn't forget that one and i didn't forget all the others
they wouldn't look at you L
they spit on you once
they spit on me once
have we all forgotten
the time you threw orange juice on me
or all the times you or max would grab me from behind
while the other threw the kick ball at me

at my face
or the time you pissed in my backpack
that was a good one
it was like fuckin lord of the flies with you guys and i was your piggy too
all the times youd step on my lunch and throw it away
yea it was good times spill
BRO
ill never forget them
theyre seared in my brain
small videos i replay over and over and over and over and over and over and over
and over and over and over and over and over and over and over and over-

L
STOP IT
STOP IT
STOP IT
why are you
why are you
why are you doing this

kel
or how about the time you and max took turns holding me down on the
playground
kicking and punching me
broke my nose
blood everywhere
here
this place
do you remember that
isn't that why they call you spill
isn't that how you got that name
blood everywhere

spill
im sorry man
it was a long time ago
i wasn't
im not
i didn't know
we were so young

kel
you went away and lost some pounds at school L
came back home and were finally pretty enough for the hot guy at school to look
at you
have you no dignity
no respect

how could you marry him

L
you need to let go
some of us aren't stuck in the past
some of us know how to forgive
some of us know how to move on

kel
keep telling yourself that L
you guys have a pretty revisionist version of our pasts
keep rewriting history

brad
i downloaded all the info on you
and mother
and everyone that came before
i saw the pictures on a now obsolete platform called facebook
and myspace
and friendster
on twitter
saw all the public things you wrote and said when you were twelve
and twenty two
and forty seven
saw the pictures
the candid snapshots
saw the people you associated with
everyone knows that who you keep close says volumes about you
you are your social circle
and the company you keep
there are no words for what they were
what you were

you thought you were only living your life
but you had already begun destroying mine
before i was even born
ive wanted to erase every part of you but it seemed like an impossible feat
doomed to this life
doomed to this fate
i would rather kill myself than keep on living

but then
the tsunami of 2037 changed everything
some have called it a tragedy
some have called it the earths way of rebelling against what we have become
a human race consumed by science and technology
the tsunami destroyed some of the memory banks on the server

whole peoples histories destroyed
gods gift for new beginnings
i am going to australia now
or what used to be australia
there i will spend all the money i have ever saved to buy a new passport
a new identity
a new history
i will buy the history of a person no longer in existence
one whose past has been destroyed by the damaged parts of the memory bank
the tsunami that came and made it possible for me to throw away my history
and become something new

spill
we can change
ive changed
it was a long time ago

kel
not long enough

L
kel

kel
congratulations on your marriage
to new beginnings
it was a beautiful ceremony
enjoy the party
                    he goes
spill
new beginnings

brad
i will erase you father
erase you from every particle of who i am
maybe this way ill have a shot at life
rewrite my history
towards a new beginning

>   *a moment as* brad *takes a deep breath*
>   *preparing for something new*
>   *preparing to say good bye*
>   *preparing for the unexpected*
>   *preparing preparing preparing*
>   L *sits on the swing*
>   *she wants to say something*
>   brad *commits*

a moment
they vanish
and then
from brad *all that comes out...*
is a tiny whimper

end of play

i wonder if it's possible to have a love affair that lasts forever
or
things i found on craigslist

by christopher oscar peña

with original music and lyrics by Melissa Lusk
   additional lyrics by christopher oscar peña

TO

Shannon Esper
Josh Barrett
Vanessa Wasche
Jennifer Ikeda
Desmin Borges
Vonian Arslanian
Lucas Near-Verbrugghe
Patrick Heusinger
Molly Ward

for making it feel like not high school

And to

Mike Donahue
Jayd McCarty

and

The Studio/New York class of 2010

for being the plays first archaelogists

and finally
FOR

Laurie Weckesser

with all my love
because she shoved me in the right direction
and cracked the world open

i wonder if its possible to have a love affair that lasts forever? or things i found on craigslist was presented by The Informers (christopher oscar peña, Artistic Director and Stephen Stout, Producing Director) in association with Avi Lipski (Producer) at Theater For a New City, New York (Crystal Field, Artistic Director) as part of the 2011 Dream Up Festival. The play opened on September 1, 2011 under the direction of Mary Birnbaum. The stage manager was Ariel C. Osborne. Daniel Zimmerman served as the Set Design Consultant, and Anshuman Bhatia did Lights.

The cast was as follows: Dax Valdes *(gino),* Sofia Gomez *(danny),* Dominic Spillane *(jon),* Stephen Stout *(eduardo),* Hannah Cabell *(mandy),* Topher Mikels *(dev),* Julia Arazi *(bruise),* Leigh Dunham *(dusk),* Michael Micalizzi *(twilight).*

A revised version of *i wonder if its possible to have a love affair that lasts forever? or things i found on craigslist* was premiered by The Informers (christopher oscar peña, Artistic Director and Stephen Stout, Producing Director) at Son of Semele, Los Angeles (Matthew McCray, Artistic Director) as part of the 2012 Company Creation Festival. The play opened on January 14, 2012 under the direction of Mary Birnbaum. The stage manager was Guillermo Parga. Ian Garrett designed lights.

The cast was as follows: Rodney To *(gino),* Rebecca Lawrence *(danny),* Gene Gallerano *(jon),* Christiina Bennett Lind *(mandy),* Scott Morse *(dev),* Lourdes Avila, Christine Corpuz, and Sam Posey *(the duendes).*

A further revised version of *i wonder if its possible to have a love affair that lasts forever? or things i found on craigslist* will premiere at the University of Illlinois- Chicago (Mary Dunford, Director of the School of Theater and Music, and Yasen Payenkov, Head of Theater) as part of their LAUNCH YEAR. Marti Lyons will direct. Opening night is set for April 11, 2014.

The cast is as follows: Alex Rodriguez *(gino),* Emily Woods *(danny),* Trace Hamilton *(jon),* Becca Brown *(mandy),* Mark Pontarelli *(dev),* Bethany Arrignton *(bruise),* David Dowd *(twilight),* Anjelica Masson *(dusk).*

CHARACTERS:

the humans

gino- *drowning in loss, weighed down by his baggage*

danny- *the symbol of perfection*

jon- *everyones dreams*

eduardo- *a guy whos lost his sense of purpose or being*

mandy- *a girl who keeps getting tripped up by her own faith*

dev- *a sweet guy with no spine*

the duendes

bruise- *a young girl with wings*

dusk- *trouble-maker on a skateboard*

twilight- *a born follower*

and the voice of facebook *and* people on facebook, *and* various strangers

SETTING:

a small town
                near the water
                                less than an hour away driving distance to a big city

TIME:

somewhere between then and this

                and back again

        for now, we'll say the years 2002 and 2012

NOTES:

-this play can be done by six actors who play each of the humans, and based on a production concept, three of those humans can double as the various duendes and random strangers. or, all the humans can play the duendes at different times, so that the duendes change physically, but keep their aura or essence. in such a production, the duendes should only be on stage when noted.

-this play can also be done with nine actors, six playing the humans, and three playing the duendes. in this case, the duendes should remain on stage almost the whole time, becoming voyeurs, like the people who read your status updates on facebook, and your wall posts to other friends- seemingly private moments exposed to a very public world.

-this is not a musical. it is a play with music. the moments of music are like soft confessionals, painful revelations. it is important that the moments feel honest and that the actors aren't trying to be showy. their voices should feel real, honest, gritty. the actors shouldn't be trying to sing the songs in the "perfect" way, but instead the songs should fit into their voices, falling out of their mouths naturally.

-things move quickly here. some moments are faster than others, but there's a sense that the ground is shifting faster than our feet can grapple with (don't take that literally). scenes should feel fluid and bleed into each other.

-a note on the duendes: feel free to play and interpret. are they fairies? spirits? ghosts? are they angels or modern mean girls? are they the inner demons of each of the human characters? are they the id or the ego? are they the voyeurs on the internet we don't even think about, staring into our lives? whatever they are to you, it is important to note the following thought in interpreting their individual character and the actions they cause:

"**duende**, like art itself, has faces that are both appealing and dangerous. it can be dark and hard to pin down."

"I never did it either. I'm not a nymphomaniac. I'm a compulsive liar."

Allison, *The Breakfast Club*

You shut your mouth
How can you say
I go about things the wrong way
I am Human and I need to be loved
Just like everybody else does

I am the son
And the heir
Of a shyness that is criminally vulgar
I am the son and heir
Of nothing in particular

How Soon is Now?, *The Smiths*

SCENE

in the darkness we hear the voices of two young men
they talk funny
their voices are clear but their grammar is fucked
they talk like theyre tripping
over numbers
in words
on the tip of their tongues

eduardo
lol
don't be such a bitch

gino
ya kno i don like shizz like that

eduardo
don't care what u like
just do it

gino
I like when u tell me what 2 do
Order me around
I like being dominated

eduardo
!!!!!!!!!!!
fuk u

gino
ima jerk off to that later

eduardo
TOOOOOOOO
MUCH
!!!!!!!!!!!!!!!!!!!!!!!

gino
me likey

eduardo
if u don't stop ima text you pictures of tits

gino
i like boobies
who doesn't like boobies?

eduardo
sending now

> *we see a picture of a naked girl pop up*
> *its not really a booby shot*
> > *its actually more like a .....*
> *COOCHIE shot*

gino
!!!!!! GROOOOOOSSSSSSSS MAN!
that's a coochie

eduardo
LOL
eat that sucka

gino
who dat be?

eduardo
some girl

gino
clearly

eduardo
wanna see more?

gino
NO

eduardo
talk to me like that again and ill blow up your phone with vaginas

gino
i hate you

eduardo
will u fuckin doIT already

gino
told u don't want 2

eduardo
PLEAZZZZZE

gino
EDDY

eduardo
U R SO AFRAID OF TECHNOLOGY
<u>WE LIVE IN DA FUTURE!!!!!!!</u>

gino
I look like ass rite now

eduardo
ive seen you roll out of bed fuckin drunk after you PUKED on urself
<u>PUKED</u>

gino
FINE

eduardo
win
BIG WIN

                  AN INTERRUPTION:
                      the duendes appear

bruise
NO ONE LOVES YOU MORE THAN ME
NO
NO ONE LOVES YOU MORE THAN ME

twilight
WELL, NO ONE ASKED YOU WHAT YOU THOUGHT
OH, NO ONE ASKED YOU WHAT YOU THOUGHT
OH, NO ONE ASKED YOU WHAT YOU THOUGHT
CAUSE YOUR THOUGHTS ARE DUMB, YEAH YOUR THOUGHTS ARE DUMB

                      and maybe here
                         everyone appears
                in their own
                    little
                        world

twilight and dusk (and company)
AND NO ONE ASKED YOU WHAT YOU WANT
AND NO ONE ASKED YOU WHAT YOU WANT
AND NO ONE ASKED YOU WHAT YOU WANT
CAUSE YOU ALREADY GOT EVERYTHING

HEY! HEY! HEY!

                eduardo *and* gino *appear in individual pools of light*
                  they talk normally now, but every once in a while a
word

or two

      drops

          out

                 fuckin skype

eduardo
I SEE YOU!

gino
are you in your underwear?

eduardo
thought youd like that

gino
you haven't even showered today have you?

eduardo
shut it

gino
your hairs so long
you look different
like a kid
when are you gonna come visit me?

eduardo
i don't know
soon
maybe next month

gino
you keep saying that
you always say that!

eduardo
shouldn't have moved three thousand miles away then huh?

gino
you should move here

eduardo
i cant

gino
you aint doing shit!
whatever shit you're doing back home you can do here

eduardo
maybe

gino
why not?!

eduardo
im afraid of change

gino
its good for you
its really really good for you
new perspective
youll look at the world in a whole new way
you've never leave home
no one ever leaves home
LEAVE
come here

eduardo
ill think about it

gino
yea yea
you're so fuckin unmotivated

eduardo
can we not fight right now please?
thanks

gino
im just sayin
you've been saying that for years

eduardo
I miss you too okay

gino
okay

eduardo
when are you gonna come home
visit
its been a while

gino
soon

eduardo
ill take you to the gay bar
get you laid
be your straight bait

gino
i want something substantial
it feels like time you know

eduardo
don't you love skype

gino
its not so bad

eduardo
hey

gino
what?

eduardo
I SEE YOU!

SCENE

danny's *office*
it is obnoxiously meticulous
like OCD perfect
everything is in its proper place
youd never believe an actual human being sometimes
inhabited this place

danny *sits at her desk conceiving a building*
after a moment
there is a knock at the door

danny
come in

mandy *stands in the doorway*
she's tan, unkempt, hair a mess
shes wearing khaki shorts, high, thick socks, and
boots
she totally looks likes she might be a lesbian but shes totally
not
she's also really dirty, not that lesbians are dirty, but you
know
mandy *clearly spend time in the dirt*
a lot of it

mandy
im here early

without looking up

danny
no problem
im almost done
take a seat

mandy
i don't want to touch anything

danny
you don't have to touch anything just
sit
sit
ill only be a moment longer
don't want to break my focus

mandy
i thought we could go down to the pier

i know youre not all outdoorsy and stuff
so we can go that restaurant on the waterfront
im really craving clam chowder for some reason

danny
as long as theres AC

mandy
i don't know how you work in this office

danny
i don't know how you work in yours

mandy
i don't really have an office

danny
exactly

        danny *finally looks up*
danny
ready
oh jesus mandy you look a mess

mandy
save me the speeches

danny
id give you a hug but –

mandy
yea

        danny *points at herself*
danny
control

        and then at mandy

danny
chaos

mandy
we're different people

danny
you can say that again

i build things
you play with dirt

mandy
oh fuck off

danny
why you became an archaeologist ill never understand

mandy
theres beauty in finding lost things danny
lost cultures
lost people
theres beauty in touching history
touching things that are hundreds
NO THOUSANDS of years old
theres beauty in finding something that's been buried for years
lost for who knows how long
and see it survive
theres beauty in that
in understanding something we never even knew was there

danny
i just don't like the idea of being stuck in the past

mandy
you say that

danny
whats that supposed to mean?

mandy
nothing

danny
im all about the future mandy
even now
i sit here
Drawing
Constructing
Imagining the future
Imagining what something can become

mandy
you just build things because you like the sense of control

danny

at least im honest about it
by the way
i told you i wanted to pay for your honey moon as my gift
have you figured out where you want to go?

mandy
greece maybe

danny
don't tell me-
theres some site you want to go to

mandy
it makes me happy

danny
where does dev want to go?

mandy
hes complacent
he doesn't really care
i'll just tell him to pack his bags and he will

danny
look whos about control now
stones in glass houses

mandy
i don't control him
its just the way he is

danny
hes just the kind of man you've always been attracted to

mandy
or there just the types of guys that are attracted to me
i know you're not religious or anything-

danny
i said id be your maid of honor but youre not making me read some fuckin bible
passage are you

mandy
i wouldn't dream of it

danny
good

mandy
do you believe in "bashert"

danny
what does that mean?

mandy
when I was ordering the cake
this little old jewish lady
she told me that dev was my bashert
i guess it's the Yiddish word for destiny
and it refers to youre
Divinely
Foreordained match
your soulmate essentially
do you believe in that?

danny
it's a nice thought
but I like my free will

mandy
sometimes
i don't know if it will last
but for now
he makes me feel like I could do anything I ever dreamed

danny
clam chowder?

<u>**SCENE**</u>

an indiscriminate living room
in an indiscriminate house
on an indiscriminate block
at an indiscriminate time
JON *sits on the couch nursing a beer*
a handsome guy in his twenties
he wears a generic suits, sans blazer, ruffled, untucked
he sits next to EDUARDO *who is sitting in his boxers, hair a*
mess

destroying hookers and pimps
in gran turismo

jon
dude
is it my turn yet?

eduardo
you know the rules man

jon
it's definitely my turn

eduardo
you got here ten minutes ago

jon
yea

eduardo
and what are the rules

jon
ed-

eduardo
what are the rules man?

jon
a gamer gets uninterrupted bad ass play time for 45 minutes

eduardo
key word being:
UNINTERRUPTED

jon
you have definitely been playing for more than 45 minutes

eduardo
how you know that?

jon
because youre SITTING exactly where i left you EIGHT hours ago

eduardo
you don't know that

jon
right

eduardo
besides the time starts when you get here
otherwise we'd be having all kinds of chaos
people calling next and then leaving for hours and making all sorts of demands
upon their returns
no way
this way is simple
rules are rules

jon
whatever
wait till summer comes and im not in school anymore
ill be sitting here all day

eduardo
ill be right here next to you calling NEXT

> *the sound of a knock at the door*
> *no one does anything*
> *another knock*

jon
you expecting someone?

eduardo
nope

jon
me neither

> *a louder more frantic knock*

eduardo
you gonna get that?

jon
you're closer to the door

the sound of keys in the door

jon
that must be danny

eduardo
shes got keys

jon
yo danny sees you haven't moved and shes gonna have your balls

eduardo
danny can lick my nuts

jon
you wish

> *the front door opens and* DANNY *stands in the doorway*
> *she's holding a Costco sized box of milk*
> *mail in her mouth*
> *and other groceries abound*
> jon *jumps up to help*

danny
are you assholes deaf or what
what the hell is wrong with you

eduardo
im in the middle of a game
jons the one that was being lazy

danny
I can see that

jon
im sorry

> jon *leans in to kiss* danny

danny
why don't you help me with all this shit first

jon
sorry

danny
yea

danny and jon *carry things into the kitchen*

eduardo
hey danny
I left my rent check on the counter

danny
I got it

eduardo
cool

danny
but youre a hundred short

eduardo
what?

danny
told you rents going up

eduardo
no you didn't

danny
yes I did

eduardo
when?

danny
i believe i yelled
if you motherfuckers don't clean this place up
im going to hire a maid and you're all going to pay an extra bill

eduardo
thought you were joking

danny
gross
put some pants on

jon
ha ha

eduardo
do that again jon-

jon
im not in charge

> danny *turns off the playstation*

eduardo
what the hell?

danny
im not joking anymore
get it together

eduardo
what are you, my mom now?

danny
mom is who you're gonna be with
when i call her and tell her shes footing the bill for you to be here
and you're not even taking the LSATS like you said you would

eduardo
you wouldnt

danny
watch me

eduardo
I dare you

jon
I wouldn't do that if I were you

> *A stand off*

eduardo
.....

danny
.....

eduardo
.....

> eduardo *caves*

eduardo
fine
but you know you're a bad sister right

danny
yea yea yea

eduardo
you know I cant take the LSATS right now
you know ive lost my sense of purpose

danny
youre just lazy

eduardo
tell er jon

jon
no way

> danny *gets on her lap top*
> *the* duendes *appear forming a triangle around*
Eduardo
> *one opens its mouth*
> *something beautiful falls out*
> *cracking* eduardo *opens*

eduardo
i wake up every morning
and I have no idea what I want to do
do I want to go to law school or move to france?
am I meant to be a doctor or a painter?
and im terrified of dad
i cant even talk to him about shit like this
could you imagine what he would say to me?
"i came to this country twenty years ago with nothing
no education
not even a high school diploma
an immigrant with only the clothes on his back
and a woman to call my wife!
and now I am a made man
living the American dream

driving a corolla when I could drive a porsche
because I worked hard
i am the american dream!
And what about you?
you who has the benefit of everything!"
my father gets to be the american dream
and I-
with no purpose
what am I with no purpose?
without a trajectory
im not even a man
you know

but no one is actually listening

danny
oh my god

jon
what

danny
did you see this thing
on facebook
this note
you were both tagged in it

jon
what?

danny
wilson chin sent out a message

wilson chin *appears*

twilights as THE VOICE OF FACEBOOK (as wilson chin)
hey guys
so it turns out our class president is out of the country
SO
im creating this facebook event to get the ball rolling on our ten year reunion
lets get some RSVPS going and plan the best decade reunion ever
lots of drinks and dancing?
open to suggestions
leave your ideas on the wall below and lets get moving
cant wait to see all you motherfuckers!
wilson

Wilson *vanishes*

eduardo
whoa

jon
it's been ten years already?

eduardo
ten years and im still the same

jon
nine for you eduardo
you weren't actually in our class

danny
yea
you were just a hanger on-er

eduardo
that's not true
im honorary
everyone said so
it was even in the yearbook

jon
only cuz your older sister was hot
and cool

danny
thanks babe
                              they kiss
eduardo
gross
get a room

danny
wilson chin
that's a name i haven't heard in a while

jon
wilson?
he and I were really close back in the day

danny
I remember

eduardo
different time
different place
same person

danny
i wonder who's going to be there
we keep in touch with most anyone who mattered

eduardo
ten years-
it sounds a lot longer when you say it out loud

jon
i always thought we'd get invitations or something
you know
Cards

danny
well we live in the modern age
things like that are-
well-
obsolete

jon
what do you ever think happened to all those people

danny
lets hope they all come so we can find out

eduardo
i wonder if they'll look different

jon
id rather not see all of those people

danny
why not?
wont it be nice
don't you think itll be nice
to say
look what became of you
and look what became of me

jon
i don't have that need

danny
what need?

jon
i don't need their approval

danny
its not about approval
its about-
checking in

eduardo
how come
i thought
aren't we supposed to feel different
you know
after ten years?
i don't feel different

jon
i don't think we should bother with this
its making eduardo anxious

danny
ANXIOUS
eduardo are you anxious
you're not anxious are you eduardo

eduardo
do you think
is it too late to apply to law school
maybe i can still send in an application
that way i can say
i can say im going to attend law school
right?

danny
absolutely
this is exactly what you need
motivation
and pants

jon
i don't know about this danny

eduardo
im going to go lie down

danny
im going to confirm us on the event invite

> danny *gets on her lap top*
> *she gets on facebook*
> *the sound of a status update (spoken by a duende)*

FACEBOOK STATUS UPDATE
Danny plus two will be attending SC High's C/O 2002 ten year reunion

jon
it's going to be people you don't even like

danny
im counting on it

jon
if we wanted to see them we would make time for them

danny
i know
this is why this is so great
we can see them all in one go

FACEBOOK STATUS UPDATE
danny is excited for her ten year reunion

jon
it's a big world out there
you know
sometimes that gets away from you
sometimes we forget
i like my little world
deaths and funerals
weddings and babies
high school reunions
i don't know
they pull things in
collide into your world
things begin to bleed into each other
you know
im not so sure i like that
id rather keep things at bay

SCENE

gino *is packing, getting ready to head back*
back
back
back
where he came from
or maybe...
hes already midflight

gino

OH GET ME OUTTA THIS TOWN
I AM AN ANIMAL
KNUCKLES DRAGGIN' ON THE LINOLEUM
STUMBLIN AROUND
LIKE I GOT SOMETHING' TO SEE HERE

PLEASE BUST ME OUTTA THIS CAGE
I AM AN ANIMAL
TALONS SCRATCHIN' ON THE LINOLEUM
CLAWIN' AT THE GROUND
LIKE I GOT SOMEWHERE TO BE HERE

HAHA HA
HAHA HA
HAHA HA

SCENE

> dev *and* mandy *sit in their living room*
> *he sits on the couch with his head in his hands*
> *she looms over him*

mandy
we're engaged

dev
this is just a hypothetical

mandy
a hypothetical engagement?

dev
QUESTION
a hypothetical question

> mandy *uses her fingers to quote everything aggressively*

mandy
so you're asking me
a "hypothetical" question
where you've "hypothetically" asked me to marry you
and now you're "hypothetically" having second thoughts
"hypothetical" cold feet as some would say
and so you want to know what I "hypothetically" think
about your "hypothetical" cold feet

dev
some thing like that

mandy
invitations have been sent out dev
rooms have been reserved
food has been ordered
I HAVE A DRESS DEV

dev
I told you not to rush into-

mandy
You ASKED me
it's not exactly rushing in when you ask

dev
you pressured-

mandy
I did what?

> mandy *grabs a plate, or maybe a glass, maybe a real cool*
> *porcelain something sitting on the mantle piece and*
> *smashes it to the ground*

dev
JESUS MANDY

mandy
JESUS IS OUT TODAY DEV

dev
this isn't-

mandy
THIS ISN'T WHAT

dev
i mean give me a break for a second

> *she SMASHES something else*

mandy
that enough of a break for you?

dev
i'm just thinking-

mandy
THAT wasn't always your strong suit now was it

dev
HEY NOW

mandy
you should leave that to me

dev
you're making me feel small mandy
we talked about this
you promised you wouldn't belittle me
make me feel like a child
I'm a grown
I'm a-

mandy
a what DEV
a WHAT?

dev
A GROWN MAN

> *silence*
> *silence*
> *silence*
> *the kind of silence that frightens you*

> *in the silence*
> *we hear* bruise *and* twilight *whispering to* mandy
> duende *whispers*

twilight
how long has he been thinking this?

dusk
silence

twilight
silence

dusk
silence

dev
will you say something

> *she doesn't*
> *she begins to pick up the broken pieces*

dev
please

> *more deafening silence*

dev
mandy
i feel safer in the chaos
I feel safer in the screaming and the smashing and the thunder
and the cries
your high pitched voice is lovely
your screams hurdle chariots with men in gold outfits and bronze spears
aimed at my gullet
i can sleep in the chaos

it lulls me to sleep
but your silence is
your silence
                    a whisper
it terrifies me

mandy
whats a gullet?

dev
what?

mandy
a GULL-ET dev
what. is. a. gull. et.

dev
i don't-
it's a-
i'm not-

mandy
you DON'T-
IT'S a-
I'M NOT-
is all that you are made of
you are made of words that don't exist

dev
a gullet is a-
is a

mandy
go to sleep dev
rest on it
do more of that "thinking" thing you're doing
you want to be a man
but the only part of a man inside you
is the one I bring to the table

dev
i want to sleep with another woman

                    this is the first real wound in mandy's armor
mandy
ANOTHER woman
this better be another "hypothetical" DEV

dev
i think we're past the hypothetical-

mandy
i will rip out your tongue dev so help me god

dev
your bark is bigger than your bite mandy
im smart enough to know that

mandy
who is she?

dev
no one in particular
just the idea

mandy
you'll throw everything away for an idea

dev
I do love you

mandy
not as much as you love yourself

dev
im sorry
                    in one quick motion
                            mandy *reaches out*
                    and grabs dev's *throat with her hand*

mandy
a gullet is an esophagus
its your throat you asshole
i think it's best if you stay somewhere else tonight

                    she lets him go

SCENE

an indiscriminate café in an indiscriminate location
the kind of places you tell your friends you wouldn't be
caught dead in-

yet you're secretly comforted by its anonymity
by its acceptance from the masses
the sound of a woman talking too loudly on the phone
cuz you know, she owns the place
the sound of a bum asking for change
or maybe hes just a hipster railing against the man
the sound of a baby crying
cuz theyre everywhere
the sound of Americans on break
san francisco, new york, chicago?
who cares
middle america

amidst all this we see gino.

gino *is probably a sweet guy but you wouldn't know it*
because you've never hung out with him before
he's not the type of guy with a ton of friends
maybe he's a little on the heavier side
or hasn't quite figured out how to handle that frizz
or maybe some might thinks he's actually attractive
if it weren't for his speech patterns, or his bad breath
or his obnoxious laugh
he's always missed something
always a little bit askew
you can't decide if he's 15 going on 27
or 23 going on 45....
he holds a cup of coffee and looks around-
he looks... uncomfortable

and then Danny *shows up*
Danny *is-*
well you know, all american perfect
on the phone with bags

danny
i told you
im not taking that job
its not big enough
its not-
its not-
are you listening to me?

271

im not designing a fuckin mall-
i don't care if its in abu fuckin dhabi
its still a mall

she hangs up

did you order me something?

no answer

did you order me something?

still no answer

GINO

gino
oh sorry
youre talking to me?

danny
who else would I be talking to

gino
oh

danny
so did you

gino
what

danny
order me something?

gino
was I supposed to?

danny
never mind
i dont need to be wired too early
so

gino
what

danny
hi

gino
hi

danny
it's good to see you!

gino
been a year or two

danny
really?
felt like a few months
time's going by so fast these days

gino
yea

danny
welll

gino
you look good

danny
do i?

gino
you always look good
i always had the most beautiful best friend

danny
thanks sweetie
so do you

gino
i do?

danny
yea
absolutely
yes
....
you look tan

gino
ive been indoors for the last month

danny
oh

gino
yea

danny
but you look great!

gino
okay

danny
so listen i totally forgot i had made dinner plans
we're having people over
this is what happens when i don't put things in the blackberry

gino
oh

danny
so i figured you should just come over
see everyone
will you?

gino
i cant

danny
oh come on
why not?

gino
i have other plans

danny
change them

gino
i cant

danny
gino!

gino
another time

i promise
im here indefinitely
been here for a month already

danny
a month?
what

gino
yes
yes yes
my mom died

danny
oh shit
sweetheart
shit
wow
shit
sorry
im sorry
do you need a hug?

gino
its okay

danny
why didn't you say anything sooner?

gino
I tried calling

danny
you did?

gino
but you were busy

danny
I was busy

gino
I understand

danny
how?

gino
car accident I think
or cancer

danny
well which is it?

gino
I don't know
Maybe both?
I didn't ask any questions when they called me

danny
they?

gino
the morgue
or the coroner
or a friend of hers
i don't really know
someone
i didn't ask too many questions
i just said "okay"
"okay"
and hung up the phone
and then I went back to my book

danny
what book?

gino
i don't remember

danny
sorry

gino
but that's not why I wanted to talk to you

danny
its not?

gino
no

danny
okay

gino
i wanted to ask you
about architecture

danny
what about it?

gino
I think I want to try it

danny
oh sweetie
its not something you just try
you have to go to school for it
you have to be really very
really smart
you have to be motivated
and applied
and it takes
trust me it takes years and years of learning
and time
the amount of time
you can't even believe the amount of commitment
and focus and time

gino
i have time
i have nothing but time
i can study
i can apply myself
i can learn something new
i can learn to be something new
im still young
we're still young

danny
its not just that G
you also
its an art you know
architecture
its an art
you have to be born with it
IT
you know IT
the big IT
Vision

you have to be a visionary
you have to see things that no one else can see
things
like

gino
like what

danny
things G

gino
i see things
you're my best friend danny
you don't think i have it

danny
gino

gino
you can tell me the truth
you would tell me the truth right?

> danny *makes bold gestures with her hands*

danny
its just
just
when you look at the sky
at space
you have so see like
like ideas
and pictures
beautiful metaphors
edges that are
you know
DIFFERENT

gino
all i see when i look at the sky is the sky

danny
yea

gino
i don't have it

danny
i mean im not saying that but-

gino
I don't have it

>   *the phone rings*
>   danny *takes it*

danny
what
how much more?

gino
how am I supposed to build a life for myself
when I don't even have it
IT
the thing that keeps me being one step short of whole
a mound of flesh with no corpse to fit around
a pulsing heart
with no love to give
a blue bird with no song
the earth with no sun
a room with no structure
a dead mother i never even knew
gino
a voice with no words

>   *there is a terrible shift*
>   *something terrifying- an explosion?*
>   *a flash?*
>   *not everyone feels it*

dusk
WE WERE ROOTED HERE ONCE

bruise
GROUNDED

dusk
WE CAME FROM THE EARTH
WE CAME FROM THE SOIL
EVEN IF WE CAME FROM MILLIONS OF COSMIC THINGS
EVEN IF WE CAME FROM GODS
WE STILL CAME FROM THE SAME THING

bruise
AND YET

dusk
NOW
NOTHING
I REMEMBER A TIME WHEN

bruise
WHEN

dusk
I REMEMBER A TIME WHEN

bruise
WHEN

dusk
SHIT
IVE FORGOTTEN

danny
were you saying something?

gino
....

SCENE

eduardo *stands on the brink of the edge*

eduardo
i wasn't ever the best student
but I certainly wasn't stupid
i mean im not dumb
i just maybe don't apply myself as much as I should
i do understand things
i just-
to understand things it sometimes helps to break them apart
to understand things fiber by fiber
to go from molecule to atom
maybe if I broke myself apart enough times-
i could find out who it is that I am

that seems easy enough
so lets define the terms of engagement
something is lost
                    eduardo *pulls out his iPhone*
          googles dictionary.com and looks up the word "lost"
                    the duendes scoff at this
                              appear
                    and help him remember
          they help him remember hes smarter than that
                    its all in his head
                         its always been there
                    before he allowed the future to cripple him

which is to say that something is not possessed or retained
or more easily
that something cant be found

as opposed to lost
in terms of being defeated or destroyed

and as opposed to lost
meaning preoccupied
rapt or distracted

now what have I lost?
myself
the simplest thing
but that's not specific enough
i have lost-
i have lost-
i have lost IDENTITY

MY IDENTITY

identity
identity
the condition of being oneself or ITSELF
and not another
that is to say I am me
but not someone else
that's not helpful enough
identity
identity
the state or fact of being one as described
being one as described

bruise
WE LIVE ON THE BRINK
AT THE EDGE OF-
DARKNESS-
AT THE EDGE OF-
A GREAT FALL-
AT THE EDGE OF-
UNDERSTANDING-
AT THE EDGE OF-
AT THE EDGE OF-
AT THE EDGE
NO LONGER SATISFIED

AT THE BRINK
IS WHERE WE LIVE ARMS
OUT STRETCHED TOES
STRESSING UNDER
THE PRESSURE OF-
LIMBS CRYING FOR THE SAFETY OF-
FOR THE SAFETY OF

YOU WERE SAFE ONCE
WE WERE SAFE ONCE
SAFETY GOT OLD
LIMITATIONS NEEDED TO BE PUSHED
BOUNDARIES HAD TO BE BROKEN
MOMENTS HAD TO BE LOST
YOU EVEN PUSHED YOURSELF OUT OF YOUR OWN BODY
UNSATISFIED
UNTIL ALL THAT IS LEFT
IS LIMBS PLEADING
STRETCHING
FOR THE ONE THING LEFT AT THE EDGES OF YOUR FINGERTIPS

eduardo
i have to find the facts that make me
the pieces
the real one

eduardo *vanishes into himself*

SCENE

a mellow happy hour at the kind of bar where people go to get drunk

this is the first and final location of the night before going home to bed

jon *and* dev *enjoy whiskey and an occasional glance at a* stranger

dev
have another

jon
i cant
im already pretty wasted

dev
you're not if you know it

jon
i should be responsible
a responsible adult

dev
come on
its still early

jon
whats in it for me

dev
the honor of my presence

jon
i think that ones been cashed out

dev
you're not going to make me sit here and drink all alone right
just me and the jukebox
some dead crooner in the background
that would officially make me an alcoholic

jon
we wouldn't want that to happen

dev
exactly

jon
alright
ill stay for another

dev
or two

jon
don't push it

dev
ill take what i can get

jon
i only drink this way when im with you

dev
sounds like a personal problem

jon
dannys always working and eduardos-

dev
still a bitch

jon
i was going to go with broke
nut that too
seen him lately?

dev
no-
its been a while

jon
you should come over some time

dev
for video games?
No thank you

jon
come on

dev
nothing against him
but he was always your friend

not mine

jon
guess not

dev
yo she is smoking

jon
who

dev
corner
next to the juke box

jon
she's alright

dev
id touch it

jon
im sure you would

dev
I WOULD

jon
I know

dev
damn right

jon
not much you wouldn't touch

dev
hey now!

jon
like back in the day

dev
shut up

jon
you still?

dev
sometimes

jon
NO
Even with mandy?

dev
it is what it is

jon
ever worry people will find out

dev
these days
who hasn't

jon
why do you still do it?

dev
i have my reasons

jon
boredom?

dev
something like that

jon
what else is there?

dev
necessity

                    jon *laughs*

jon
right
it's a necessity

dev
IT IS

jon
okay

dev
im serious

jon
whatever
no judgement

dev
you don't understand

jon
understand what

dev
mandy and I don't have sex

jon
what?

dev
we don't have sex

jon
how often does that mean

dev *make a zero with his hands*

jon
i mean you shouldn't be marrying someone who doesn't put out
you can still get out you know
im just saying
this shouldn't be happening right now

dev
its not like that

jon
that's what it sounds its like
i mean how long-
like its been a week
or a month
or six months
or a year

dev
never

jon
NEVER

dev
never

jon
never?
I don't understand

dev
SHES A VIRGIN
We're virgins

jon
Holyshityourejokingright

Hes NOT joking

jon
no wonder you're still getting hand jobs from strangers

dev
it's a necessity

jon
ill bet it is

dev
thank god for the internet

SCENE

gino *gets on facebook*
he's never been on facebook before

gino
it turns out i am a masochist
it turns out that everything ive ever run away from
i welcome back with open arms
because after escaping it for seven years
i decide to get on facebook
actually get on
i mean of course ive searched though it
snuck glances at people i sometimes wonder about
but for the first time I actually create an account
a real one
i take a picture of myself to upload

gino *takes a picture of himself*
hes unhappy with it
so he
takes another
and another
and another and another and another
until
he
takes
the right one

satisfactory
i upload it
and immediately
i realize
i never actually thought id ever see any of these people again
not in a concrete real way
i thought theyd always remain a distant image
fading more and more and more each day
i thought
thought id move away
far away
no return address
never have to see their faces
distant nightmares left behind in a field of shattered memories
things I thought
people I thought
were gone forever
buried
and now

here they were

twilight as THE VOICE OF FACEBOOK (as wilson chin)
wilson chin

wilson chin appears

gino
still living in our old neighborhood

twilight as THE VOICE OF FACEBOOK (as wilson chin)
B.A. from cal poly, san luis obispo in computer science
married to tina tran

gino
and

bruise as THE VOICE OF FACEBOOK (as stanley barron)
stanley barron

stanley barron appears

gino
engaged to that bitch erin fischer

bruise as THE VOICE OF FACEBOOK (as Stanley Barron)
employed by p g and e

gino
well that's not surprising
he was always hot but there wasn't much there

dusk as THE VOICE OF FACEBOOK (as sonia vazquez)
sonia vazquez

gino
she was always sweet
she once shared her lunch with me

dusk as THE VOICE OF FACEBOOK (as sonia vazquez)
single
currently attending community college

gino
three kids
i scroll through her pictures
theyre beautiful
her children
and im struck by the fact
that I haven't seen this woman for ten years

and yet some how
im seeing every intimate detail of the last decade
her son in a pool
her daughter eating ice cream
sonia as a bridesmaid
a night out drinking
oh- an unflattering angle

we see some of these moments
maybe the duendes show them to us

the access makes me nervous
the access makes me excited
the access terrifies me

he gets off facebook and the voices disappear
and yet
i cant stop looking
and I can't help but wonder
what it was all like before
before the future arrived
the past stayed in the past
because people could move away
because people could become different people
and disappear forever
facebook
what were we like without the social network
that must have been a luxury
facebook
maybe somewhere deep inside
in a network of pictures and words
in a network of digital memories
i can get lost

SCENE

danny and jon *sit in bed, late at night*

danny
i know you think going to this reunion is
i don't know
unnecessary or foolish
but it's important to me
it is
and I just
i want you to take it seriously

jon
i always do
whatever you say
i always do
i don't ask questions

danny
okay
good
yea
that's great

jon
but this
jus tell me why

danny
i said

jon
no you didn't
not really
no

danny
i want to see what people turned out like

jon
its more than that
if you say it
ill drop it

danny
i want every one to see

i want them to see you
to see me
to see you with me

jon
but nothings changed

danny
what do you mean

jon
if you'd been ugly in school
unpopular or fat or unliked
if people had made fun of you and put gum in your hair
and made you cry
if you had been belittled and crushed
i could understand this need
it wouldn't make it right
or any better
but i could understand it
this need to say
"i turned out better than you
i did"
or
or
or
"i survived"
but you didn't
that wasn't you
you were always the OTHER girl
its like pissing on territory that's already yours

danny
it's just

jon
what?
          a shift
                    jon *gets out of bed*
                         he runs
                              and runs
                                   and runs and runs
                         repeating something over and over to himself
jon
the love of my life is ugly
the love of my life is ugly
the love of my life is ugly

the love of my life is ugly

        as he runs
      we see:

          a stranger *get into a parked car with* dev

      mandy *walking around in her wedding dress*

           eduardo *standing in front of a*

wall

         the wall has pictures of people
          notes on yellow pieces of paper
            post-its
        things pinned to string that hang

aimlessly

          he studies them searching
            searching
             searching

     danny *chases after* jon

       the sound of dev *climaxing in a car*

      jon *keeps running*

    gino *appears and trips* danny

jon
the love of my life is ugly

dusk
SHES JUST LIKE YOU

<u>**SCENE**</u>

eduardo *and* mandy
theyre texting

eduardo
im sorry this is happening-

mandy
i don't want to talk about it

eduardo
im just saying-

mandy
i know

then
chatting online

eduardo
im collecting things

mandy
things?

eduardo
found objects
old songs ive forgotten on mix tapes
notes left behind in the pockets of jeans
love letters folded into origami for extra protection
faded photographs stowed away in velcro wallets
with the logos of old british rock groups
forgotten lovers
things that make me who I am
history

mandy
you shouldn't do that

eduardo
it's fun
you find things youd forgotten
like this

he e-mails her an old photograph of them sitting in a treee

eduardo

an old photograph of us
sitting in a tree
a forgotten moment
lost in the ether
but captured right here
it's like reliving it all over again
experiencing the same pleasant surprise

mandy
not so pleasant

eduardo
no?
                    and then they meet in real life
                              they eat cotton candy
                                    from the pier
                                          or the boardwalk
                    from childhood

mandy
you shouldnt dredge up the past
its not so pleasant for all of us

eduardo
sorry
i thought it would bring back a nice memory

mandy
we haven't spoken in-
god knows how long

eduardo
you told me not to call you
you said
"i never want to see you ever again"

mandy
well you should have

eduardo
that's so confusing
why does everything have to mean something else
why cant everything just be what it is?

mandy
it never is

eduardo
why did you break up with me?

mandy
lets not relive this okay

eduardo
im just trying to understand myself
through moments
but I don't understand all of the moments so-

mandy
this isn't a good time for me

eduardo
okay

mandy
i keep getting left behind
by men
by people im supposed to trust
by people I give my heart to

eduardo
i didn't leave you behind
you asked me to leave

mandy
you were being insensitive
you were an asshole
you didn't respect my my my
my
needs

eduardo
the same could be said for you

mandy
so we're incompatible

eduardo
so it seems

mandy
this is all making me feel so crazy
i swear
i am a peaceful person who is filled with violent rage

eduardo
you weren't like that with me

mandy
oddly enough
when youre not being a dick
you have a remarkable way of
youre
soothing
youre soothing
you calm me

eduardo
im glad

mandy
yea
so what have you discovered about yourself

eduardo
i don't know

mandy
there must be something
an item from your list

eduardo
ill tell you one if you tell me one

mandy
okay

eduardo
sometimes i leave poetry in library books

mandy
i didn't know you did that

eduardo
nobody does

mandy
except for me

eduardo
except for you

so whats yours

mandy
im afraid its not so charming

eduardo
being charming is easy
embracing yourself-
that's brave it turns out
so what is it?

mandy
nothing i believe in makes sense anymore

SCENE

danny *is having a nightmare*
or a dream
or maybe shes living in a fucked up fantasy
she appears in a sexy nightgown and sings a song and dances a
dance
its like a stilted cabaret

danny
YOU SHOW ME YOURS AND I WILL SHOW YOU MINE
I GOT THE AFTERNOON FREE
AND IT WOULD BE SO NICE TO UNWIND
OH

YOU SHOW ME MINE AND I WILL SHOW YOU YOURS
I GOT A WHOLE LOTTA TIME
AND I CAN BET YOU WILL WANT MORE
OH

EVERY SINGLE DAY
FEELS LIKE MY MOUTH IS KEEPIN MY HEART AT BAY
OH

EVERY SINGLE NIGHT
SOMETHIN DON'T FEEL RIGHT

SCENE

dev has just climaxed in a car
a random guy *(twilight)* sits next to him

random guy
did you like that?

dev
sure

random guy
just sure

dev
I have no complaints

random guy
we should do this again some time

dev
maybe

random guy
can I get your number?
you're cute

dev
email me

random guy
okay
whats your name?

dev
lookingforrelease@gmail.com

random guy
funny

dev
it aint supposed to be funny

random guy
okay then

dev pulls out a wad of cash

throws the random guy *a twenty*

random guy
whats this?

dev
for your troubles

random guy
i don't need it
im not doing this for the money
im doing it because I want to
your post didn't say anything about money

dev
just take it

random guy
im not a fuckin prostitute

dev
no?
well at the very least-
you're a fuckin whore

random guy
FUCK YOU MAN

random guy *gets out of the car and slams it shut HARD*

dev
i feel so lonely I could die

SCENE

gino appears

gino
being on facebook for the first time
is like picking at a scab over and over and over again
oddly enough
i don't feel so lonely
oddly enough
i feel like all these people are here with me
their intimate lives so close to me I can touch them
and then
and then something else happens
i see him
and I can't
i cant breathe

dev appears

dev as THE VOICE OF FACEBOOK (as Dev Barlow)
dev barlow

gino
i reopen the wound

dev
dev barlow
class of 2006
b.a. university of california, san diego
engaged to mandy ronson

gino
my loneliness suffocates me
my loneliness reminds me that it is still here
my loneliness reminds me that it has taken a hold of me
and that it is never letting go
i look at Dev
i look at Dev
i look at Dev
and wonder

dev
i wonder if its possible to have a love affair that lasts forever?

the sound of water
    the sound of water just before
a really
REALLY

i mean really fuckin scary

T   s
U   n
A   m   I

and then a crash
        and then darkness
            and just silence

end of act one.

act two...

<u>SCENE</u>

> jon *is having a frenzied dream*
> *a night terror*
> *he startles*
> > *lays back down*
> > > *hes half awake....*
> > *half dreaming*
> > > *the sound of water*
> > > > *on a cool lake*
> > > > > *on a warm day*
> > *as* jon's *dream progresses*
> *the water gets rougher*
> *and rougher*
> > *and*   *rougher*
> > > *and ROUGHER*

jon
i remember this story
about this guy
he was a greek god
or a nymph
some sort of otherly mythical being type guy
otherly
is that a word?
his name was narcissus
and everyone thought he was the most beautiful thing theyd ever seen
girls wanted him
guys wanted him
he was the epitome of perfection
but narcissus
he didn't care about all this
he didn't care about anyone or anything
the way the story goes
theres this girl named echo whos in love with him
and she cant speak
or she can
but she can only repeat what someone else has already said
or something
i don't really remember
but so this guy
he pisses someone off
for some reason
and this person
i forget who
puts a spell on him

or a curse
and makes this guy fall in love with himself
so this guy sits in front of a lake
and he like looks at himself
he spends all day looking at his reflection
in love with this thing he's looking at
thinking its someone or something else
or maybe he knows its his own reflection
that parts also really unclear to me
but so this guy
that's all he does all day
he just looks and stares
and fawns
and is like genuinely happy
and in love
with this image
one day for whatever reason
he likes reaches out to the water
or tries to kiss his reflection
or something
but he falls in
this guy just falls into this lake
and well
he drowns

the water gets rougher and rougher
jon *begins to drown in it*

the thing is
the thing
im not like that you know
im not what people think I am
or maybe I was
maybe I was but im not
im not
im not anymore
i don't see what that guy did
when I look in the mirror all I see is an animal
sometimes I wish I was blind so I wouldn't have to look at myself anymore

and then there is only the sound of water

SCENE

mandy *gets on her facebook*
she takes a picture of herself in her dress using photobooth
snap

     snap

         snap

            snap

 snap

     snap

         snap

           snap

twilight as THE VOICE OF FACEBOOK
new picture uploaded
make profile picture?
profile picture selected

mandy
i should update my status
mandy wants every one to know that the wedding is off
dev is considering other options
thanks to every one who was rooting for us all these years and were hoping we
made it
i did too
asshole
this was supposed to help me feel less anxious and sad
now I feel nothing at all

SCENE

> danny *and* jon *are having sex-*
> > *it's sort of*
> *well*
> > *boring*
> > > *eventually they stop*

danny
why wont you look at me

jon
what

danny
you never look at me

jon
im looking at you right now

danny
you always-
whenever we-
theres only so much-

jon
what

danny
are we sexually incompatible?

jon
what does that even mean

danny
you never have the lights on
you always insist on turning them off
you never

jon
stop it

danny
why don't you want to see me

jon
its not that

danny
do you even know what I look like anymore

jon
can we just drop this please

danny
you used to make me feel beautiful

jon
people are either beautiful or theyre not
you don't need me to make you feel beautiful

danny
you don't do you

jon
go look in the mirror and decide for yourself
youre strong enough to do that
aren't you?
ARENT YOU?

danny
i always thought
i always thought YOU were the most beautiful thing id ever seen

jon
well that's a problem isn't it
if you love something ugly, what does that make you?

danny
don't say that

jon
i have these nightmares
and I keep trying to run from myself
but its like im not moving
im still me
and me isn't the best thing danny
me isn't the best thing to be
and if you think i am
then you have bigger problems than I could ever see

jon *gets out of bed*
danny *is motionless*

SCENE

dev *sits on the edge of the pier*
his feet dangle in the water

dev
human beings are made up of fifty five to seventy percent water
depening on their body size
no wonder it's the only place i ever feel at home
i come here often
put my feet in the water
and finally feel connected to something
i feel a part of something bigger than me
the water is sense memory to me
it reminds me of a time when I was happy
of a time when I didn't know who I was
but it didn't matter
because who I was
was still enough
everyday i imagine getting on a boat and setting sail
into the sun
waking up every day and getting into the water
and just being
to be on a boat
stowed away with the one person who-
no
i only put my feet in-
because i don't deserve the feeling of the water enveloping me
i threw that right away a long time ago

he rolls up his sleeves and looks at black ink on his arm
he rubs it
but we don't see what it is or what it says
and then the moment is broken
the sound of a phone
he answers

dev
whats up jon

Jon appears

jon
you alright man?

dev
yea why

jon
you sure?
whatever you need

311

im here

dev
what are you talking about?

jon
you and mandy

dev
what about us

jon
you didn't tell me you were calling off the wedding

dev
what?

jon
mandy posted on her facebook
her status
the wedding is off?

dev
fuck
fuck
FUCK

twilight
the sound of facebook exploding

the sound of facebook exploding

<u>**SCENE**</u>

eduardo *and* gino *hang out at home*

eduardo
how long are you planning on staying in town

gino
don't know
my tickets open ended

eduardo
i think you should stay

gino
so many different options
limitless
who knows

eduardo
whats your favorite memory of me

gino
why?

eduardo
as my best friend
i feel like what you remember about me
probably means more than what other people do
so this'll help me understand myself better
or something

gino
eating lumpia
you would come over after school
and my mother would make it

eduardo
yea!
i loved that stuff!

gino
she would never make it for me
but if I told her you were coming over
she would always have a batch ready

eduardo

that smell
i don't remember it vividly but I remember what it made me feel

gino
whats that?

eduardo
like the world was huge and there was endless possibility
it made me feel like we were on the brink of being
becoming
of doing
you know
whatever

gino
and then you grow up

eduardo
lets make lumpia

gino
what?
why?

eduardo
come on!

gino
no

eduardo
itll be fun

gino
youre so weird

eduardo
if we do it
if we get it just right
i don't know
maybe the smell will conjure the past
the smell will be like a magic trick and we'll remember that feeling
that time
COME ON

gino
i cant

eduardo
why not

gino
because I cant
literally
i don't know how
my mother never taught me
she didn't think a man should be in the kitchen
she didn't
i don't know how okay

eduardo
okay
you know my father loves you
he thinks youre motivated
he thinks I should be more like you

gino
yea
maybe
once upon a time
he just think im ethnic so he thinks i have to work extra hard or something
so he thinks i have like thicker skin and probably deserve my success more
i don't know
he probably doesn't understand that being a dick to you
is just as hurtful as some person thinking youre second class because youre
"ethnic"
but who knows
people cant ever seem to see past their own sightlines

eduardo
yea
i mean i know we're armenian and everything
but to everyone else
i just look like some white guy

gino
with pretty eyes

eduardo
aren't you sweet

gino
i remember something

eduardo
what?

gino
when we were little
you would talk like your dad

eduardo
and you would talk like your mom

gino
the accents

> *they start doing them*

gino
why you not be more manly
play sport
get out of kitchen
not for you

eduardo
i work hard to get to this country
i slave for hours
for what
worthless lazy son
useless

> *they laugh*
> *it's a little bit sad*

eduardo
i wonder if that makes us self hating
talking like that

gino
no
it just means our parents were assholes

eduardo
hey I have an idea!

gino
what?

eduardo
the internets

> eduardo *gets on google*

he pulls up a video

eduardo
TA-DA

It is a video
On youtube
of a young girl
teaching viewers
how to make lumpia

dusk
kamusta at maligayang pagnating sa aking kusina!
ngayon gumawa kami ng lumpia – sarap!

*translation:
(hello, and welcome to my kitchen!
today we make lumpia – delicious!)

SCENE

mandy is creating a craigslist post

mandy
im not as happy as i should be
so maybe
maybe now its time to do the opposite thing
so i get online
i type in the letters
craigs list dot come
i click on the personals
women seeking men
and I write a post
for the highest bidder:
wwenty eight year old female
dark curly hair
freckles
bright eyes
more importantly
to all the men out there
i am a virgin
selling it off
to the highest bidder
ready.
set.
go.
POST AD
done

she vanishes

SCENE

danny *and* gino

danny
i don't know what to do

gino
im sorry

danny
what do you think I should do?

gino
i don't know

danny
why doesn't he think im beautiful
why doesn't he see me
i just want him to see me

gino
i have to go soon

danny
don't leave me
why would you leave me when im like this
when im so fragile

gino
do you know who my first love was
or what my favorite song is
or why i moved so far from everyone
do you know when im laughing because im happy
and when im laughing because im faking it
because if i don't ill just start crying
i don't think you do
you've never been happy for me
i was your best friend in high school because i made you feel beautiful
but you never thought the college I went to was good enough
you never thought I was capable enough to accomplish anything
you never thought I was attractive or interesting
you don't know why I dropped out of school
or how lonely I can be
you don't know how much I gave up
you don't know how much I had to lie
i don't feel sorry for you anymore danny

i don't
you always had the tools to be a better person
to be the best possible person
but youre crippled by your own fear
and so instead
youre just
i don't know what you are

danny
im sorry
he's what I want
im just blinded by it

gino
did you hear anything I just said

danny
i feel incomplete gino

gino
i used to give jon hand jobs

danny
what

gino
in the bathroom

danny
I don't believe you

gino
hes definitely not gay
but he just needed to get off
you know
and i was there for that
i provided that luxury

danny
don't

gino
it was easy
just a handjob
he just closed his eyes
and it could have been anyone
it could have been you

but then again it was probably me

danny
why are you doing this

gino
he was so perfect
so beautiful
and yet
peoples base desires are just that
base
it was so easy
he was so easy to manipulate
so easy to have

danny *slaps* gino

danny
how could you

gino
feel better now?

danny
you were my best friend

gino
doesn't it feel weird now
saying those words
questioning their validity
realizing they may have been false all along

danny
get out

gino
don't kill the messenger
just thought you should know

danny
you may think im a bitch
but im at least im transparent
i don't know what YOU are

gino
now you know what it felt like to be me
maybe you should be alone for a while

figure out who you are
without everyone else

SCENE

jon *and* dev *at a bar*

dev
she wont return my calls
or my texts
her parents sent me nasty emails
her friends left me shitty comments
people i haven't spoken to in years
YEARS
some of the shit they've written me
i don't even know half you motherfuckers
what do they care anyway
stay out of my life

jon
dannys a good person
right?
but if she loves a monster
doesn't that say something about her?
i thought she was smarter than that
shes better than me right
she should be making better choices

dev
i just want to-
nothing i ever do-
the choices i-
i always end up in a corner
even when i try-
im not even happy
if im going to be-
i should at least be happy
get what i want-
its always
gino

jon
what about him
what about gino
why are you bringing up gino

dev
i really cared about him

jon

you did?
why didn't you ever say anything

dev
i think i hurt him

jon
hurt him how?

jon
badly

SCENE

mandy *and* eduardo *sitting on the pier*

eduardo
why don't you take off that dress?

mandy
it deserves to be worn

eduardo
it's a nice dress
you make a lovely bride

mandy
would have been

eduardo
are you going to take him back

mandy
no

eduardo
what if he apologizes
what if he made a mistake

mandy
i don't know how to forgive
its my biggest flaw
i understand the idea of it
the concept
but I cant emotionally
ill always look at him and remember
and itll weigh me down
and ill drown in the memory of it
so better to end it now

eduardo
starting over isn't always so bad
take it from me
apparently im still at square one

mandy *kisses* eduardo

mandy
not square one

square two
you kiss better than you used to
you have at least that

he kisses her again

mandy
lets go home together

eduardo
really

mandy
yes

eduardo
we cant

mandy
why not

eduardo
i wont

mandy
i want to

eduardo
you don't
youre just sad

mandy
im telling you I do

eduardo
not this way mandy

mandy
if you wont
someone else will

eduardo
don't say that

mandy
its true

eduardo
i already lost you once for trying to

mandy
things are different now

eduardo
it doesn't matter

mandy
come on

eduardo
NO

mandy
i have to go then

eduardo
wait why

mandy
because I have to

eduardo
stop it
don't-

mandy
im meeting someone

eduardo
who?

mandy
a guy

eduardo
what guy?

mandy
some guy

eduardo
what guy mandy

mandy

none of your business

eduardo
don't do this

mandy
some guy i met on craigslist

eduardo
craigs list?
WHAT
i don't believe you

she pulls out her blackberry
and opens her email
and shows him her post

mandy
i posted a craigs list ad
he reads it

eduardo
for the highest bidder:
twenty eight year old female
dark curly hair
freckles
bright eyes
more importantly
to all the men out there
i am a virgin
selling it off
to the highest bidder
Ready.
Set.
Go.

mandy
so you see
if you don't
someone else will

SCENE

bruise
you know
it wasn't always like this

dusk
it wasn't

twilight
really

bruise
you don't remember

twilight
no
i thought this was all there ever was

bruise
no

twilight
was it better

dusk
no
maybe
i don't know

twilight
look at them
                and we do
          you know-
              in the future that is now

      dev *texts and texts and texts*
           danny *sits in front of the camera crying*
                trying to be beautiful for it
                  failing epically
             gino *stalks on facebook*
              more and more people from his past
     reappearing
        eduardo *posts pictures of himself*
          pictures from his childhood
             pictures of his father and his mother

he scans them or takes pictures of the pictures with his
digital cam
        and he uploads them to the web
              where they will live forever
mandy *reads her craigslist post over and over to herself*
               or maybe she reads different strangers
responses
             she is digging for herself in a place where she
is a stranger
        jon *goes through his old yearbook*
          he sees pictures of himself
       and reads headlines that remind us that he is-
             the symbol of all american perfection
        he sobs while he does this

        and dusk *continues to be magical*
      meanwhile bruise *tries to dismantle the internet*

bruise
you have to remember

twilight
i cant

dusk
there has to be a way

bruise
the code
the code
the code
the code the code

                and all of a sudden something thunderous
    happens

bruise
and the internet dies
   and with it goes wikipedia
and the facebook
     and craigs list
   and your ability to find information in a flash of light
     and your ability to connect with people at a touch of a button
  and the battery on your cell phone ceases to function
     and all of a sudden you don't know what to do
because you forgot what this used to feel like
      and everyone freaks out
    they all bang on their cellphones
  and slam on their computer screens

                    and shake their cameras
                                but nothing seems to work
                        and they all
                    collectively
                    yell
            "FUCK"
        cuz now what?
    and suddenly we're thrust into the past
                        a brief moment into what things used to be like
            the year 2002
                    before all this.....

all
AND NO ONE REALLY THOUGHT THAT YOU WERE HOT
YEAH, NO ONE THOUGHT THAT YOU WERE HOT
NO, NO ONE THOUGHT THAT YOU WERE HOT
AT LEAST NOT AS HOT AS YOU THOUGHT YOU WERE

AND NO ONE THOUGHT THAT YOU WERE COOL
NO, NO ONE THOUGHT THAT YOU WERE COOL
NO, NO ONE THOUGHT THAT YOU WERE COOL
AT LEAST NOT AS COOL AS YOU REALLY WERE

AND NO ONE LOVES YOU MORE THAN ME
NO, NO ONE LOVES YOU MORE THAN ME
YEAH, NO ONE LOVES YOU MORE THAN ME
CAUSE I TELL IT TO YOU STRAIGHT, YEAH I TELL IT TO YOU STRAIGHT

HEY! HEY! HEY!

<u>**SCENE**</u>

> dev *and* gino *sit on a boat*
> *floating in a lake*
> *everything is still*
> *everything is at peace*
> gino *is writing something on* dev's *arm with a black sharpie*

gino
do you ever look at something so hard it becomes unrecognizable?

dev
what do you mean?

gino
like you stare at it so hard
for so long
it becomes foreign
like when you say a word over and over and over
a word that you know
a regular word
if you say it a lot
it starts to feel
like a made up word
like
mouth
mouth
mouth
mouth
mouth
mouth
try it

dev
mouth
mouth
mouth
mouth
mouth
mouth mouth mouth
whoa

gino
see

dev
that's weird

gino
does that ever happen when you look at something?

dev
sort of

gino
yea?

dev
when im with you
i don't recognize myself

gino
or maybe you do
but youre just not used to it

dev
yea
>   *they kiss*
>   *its tender*
>   *and awkward*
>   *and gawky*
>   *but sweet*

>   *then*
>   dev *reads the writing on his arm*

dev
i wonder if its possible to have a love affair that lasts forever
that's a deep question

gino
im a pretty deep person

dev
are you?

gino
totally
>   *they kiss*

dev
deep down inside youre just a hopeless romantic

gino
i cant take all the credit for it

dev

no?

gino
its an andy warhol quote

dev
no shit

gino
yea

dev
do you like him

gino
yea i think so
i like the idea of him
i like the idea of-
i want to
people like warhol
they seem to see the world in a different way
id like to be like that
i can relate
at least i think i can

dev
we should get back soon

gino
hey
are we-

dev
what

gino
you know

dev
what

gino
i think i know the answer
but im afraid to articulate the question
afraid to create a splash

dev

what

gino
are we together

dev
we're together right now

gino
you know what i mean

dev
why put a name on it

gino
because i need to know what it is to understand it

dev
don't be so young
you sound like a kid

gino
dev we have sex
you take me out on boat rides
wont you just say it
this is something right

dev
i can only offer so much
and i think if i'm clear about that
then its okay

gino
then be clear

dev
out here on the water
on this boat
is the most sacred place i know
i bring YOU here
not anyone else
i hold you
i feel your flesh and the muscle and bone
i taste your sweat and hear your thoughts
your loud overpowering thoughts
i share the most intimate parts of myself with you
i express things to you

and feel things for you that no one else will get to feel
ever
i am more myself than i can possibly be most days
i give all that to you
but that is all i can give
that is all i can do
i cant be more than the man i am capable of
these are my limitations
i wish we could float away on some little boat forever
land on some deserted island
just you and me
i wish this one moment would last forever
but it cant
and it doesn't
and it wont
because we cant just float out here forever
and there is no deserted island
this is what i can give you
let that be enough

gino
are you going to prom?

dev
no

gino
i was hoping we could go together

dev
don't be ridiculous

gino
i love you

dev
i know

gino
say it back

dev
gino

gino
say it back dev

dev
you know how i feel

gino
if you love me you can do this for me right
if you love me
you can take these risks

dev
my love has limitations
everyone's does

gino
what if i tell everyone

dev
you wont

gino
but what if i do

dev
id deny it

gino
youd deny everything

dev
yes

gino
you would throw everything away

dev
if you force me into that corner
yes
i would
itd be your own fault

gino
im going to tell everyone

dev
no one would believe you

gino
id make them

dev
no one would believe you gino
theyd look at you and then theyd look at me
this story could never exist in any book
theyd all just laugh at you

gino
you actually believe that don't you

dev
why cant you just let it be the way it is

gino
and then what
my mothers ashamed of me
and my boyfriend-

dev
don't say that

gino
doesn't want to acknowledge i exist

dev
this is the best i can do

gino
this isn't the future i want

dev
you always want too much
just be happy with what you have

gino
im going to tell people

dev
im sorry
you wont like what you find
                              gino *jumps into the water*
dev
gino
GINO
what are you doing
don't do this
don't

just come back

         but gino *just swims away*
             deaf to the world around him

dev
ill never be more than the sum of my parts
i think im in love
but i don't want to be
im terrified
that's all

<u>**SCENE**</u>

> mandy *and* eduardo *are in the back of* eduardo's *jeep*
> *making out ferociously*
> *its very sexy and very intense*
> *fogged up mirrors*
> *the nines*

eduardo
say that you love me

mandy
just keep kissing me

eduardo
i want to hear you say that you love me

mandy
don't be such a girl
> *he stops*

eduardo
why wont you just say it?

mandy
because

eduardo
because what?

mandy
you cant just ask someone to tell you they love you
you have to let them say it when they feel it
when they feel right

eduardo
i love you

mandy
im glad

eduardo
fuck off

mandy
that's how you speak to the woman you love

eduardo
whatever

mandy
come on
kiss me

eduardo
no

mandy
kiss me
don't be so sensitive
don't be so weak
be a man
be my strong man

she starts kissing his neck

eduardo
i hate when you do that

mandy
you love when i do that

they get it on again

eduardo
god you taste so good

mandy
i love the way you feel pressed againt me
i can feel every part of you

eduardo gets more and more aggressive

eduardo
feel every part of me

he becomes more and more aggressive
he starts to really rip her clothes off
starts taking off his pants

mandy
slow down

eduardo
come on
ill show you how strong i can be

she giggles
he powers on

eduardo
you like that

mandy
okay
i get it

you can stop now

he doesn't
he gets more and more intense about it

eduardo
come on take it

mandy
stop it eduardo
STOP IT

she SLAPS him
HARD
he stops

eduardo
OW
what the fuck is wrong with you

mandy
i told you to stop
i told you i don't want to have sex you asshole
get off me
GET OFF ME

he gets off of her

eduardo
youre such a fuckin bitch
GOD
what do you want?
I DON'T KNOW WHAT YOU WANT

mandy
i don't ever want to see you again
you animal
you fuckin monster
i hate you

she gets out of the car
pulling herself together
she runs and runs and runs
until she collapses and begins to cry

eduardo
i wish i could just walk away from myself
i don't understand anything

SCENE

danny *sits on her computer in her high school classroom*
she is working on the yearbook
she is scanning a picture of herself
she gets on her computer and signs on to the internet
the high pitch and static noise of old school modem

DIAL-UP

a few moments
an then the familiar sound of the words:
YOU'VE GOT MAIL
and then gino *appears*
he stands in the doorway
soaking wet

gino
danny

danny
gino!
youre all wet
why are you all wet
never mind
i got voted most likely to succeed
and most popular
and most athletic girl
miss mason said im not allowed to be all three in the yearbook
so i have to pick just one
but im not sure which
what do you think

gino
i haven't cried in five years
since i was a kid
i feel like the space between my throat and my stomach is missing
like someone has blown a giant hole in the middle of it
this pain
i fear it might last forever
this missing part of me
i fear it might linger
i fear i might be hollow forever

danny
youre always so dramatic
im sure its not that big of a deal
i think i should do most likely to succeed
i mean obviously id rather be most popular
but most likely to succeed just seems to have

343

you know
so much more potential
and most athletic
whatever
i can do without that
why are you all wet

gino
i swam here
i didn't know what else to do
im freezing

danny
yea you should go dry off in the gym or something
you might catch a cold
whats wrong with you
always doing such weird crazy things

gino
people say im eccentric

danny
yea
or something

gino
whats wrong with being different

danny
nothing
being different makes you special
it makes you
memorable
yea
oh you got a senior most too

gino
i did?

danny
yea

gino
which one

danny
most changed

gino
what does that even mean
most changed
from what to what

danny
eccentric to more eccentric

gino
i was hoping id change for the better

danny
you are who you are
and that isn't such a bad thing is it
youre so funny

gino
people think im funny
but i don't crack jokes to make people smile
its because im afraid of feeling their sadness

danny
heres some good news!
jon asked me to prom!
isn't that exciting?

gino
yea
exciting
totally exciting
woo hoo

SCENE

mandy *is crying on* dev's *shoulder*

dev
i don't understand

mandy
will you just hold me
just for a minute

dev
as long as you need

mandy
i thought love was supposed to be easier
i thought you just met the one
and everything would be okay
i thought it was supposed to make you happy
why aren't i happy
why is everything so complicated

dev
maybe you just haven't found the right person

mandy
i never ever want to have sex
not until im married and in love and i know
i know it's the right person

dev
maybe theres no such thing as the right person

mandy
do you think this feeling will ever go away

dev
i don't think its supposed to
i thinks it supposed to remind us of the mistakes we've made

SCENE

gino *is giving* jon *a hand job in his room*
jon's *eyes are closed*
gino's *not actually crying*
but he looks like he might start at any second
he attempts to kiss jon
jon *shoves him of hard*

jon
DUDE
what are you doing?

gino
thought you might like it

jon
fuck you dude
we had an understanding
im not fuckin gay
youre only here for one reason

gino
dev liked it

jon
yea fuckin right

gino
come on

jon
dude
im being fucking serious right now
that's isn't part of the deal
in fact im done
get the fuck outta my sight right now

gino
whats the big deal

jon
i said no

gino
i could tell everyone you know

jon

347

do it
see what happens

gino
im not afraid of pain

jon
look dude
i thought we were cool
are we cool or what

gino
maybe

jon
ill let you blow me

gino
yea?

jon
do it

gino *gets on his knees*
jon *unzips his pants*
gino *looks up*

jon
hold on a sec

gino
what?

jon
close your eyes

gino *does so*
jon *pulls out a camera*

jon
open them

as gino *opens his eyes*
jon *snaps a picture of him*

gino
what are you doing

jon
you might be able to stand the pain
but you wont be able to stand the humiliation
you say one fuckin word
ill drop this picture

all over campus
in the bathroom
sneak it in text books
locker rooms
everything

gino
its your dick in the picture

jon
no way to prove that

gino
ive been humiliated before
my whole life is a series of small humiliations

jon
not this way you haven't

gino
try me

jon
you want everyone to know what a submissive little bitch you are
desperate for cock

gino
that's not what this is

jon
you think you have some sort of connection to me because i let you fuckin touch
me
pathetic
that's something youll never have
youre just a disposable thing we use to get off on

gino
i don't care what you say
i don't care what any of them do

jon
what about your mother
how do you think she'd feel seeing a picture of her little boy
on his hands and knees
with a dick in his face

gino

you wouldn't

jon
a pictures worth a thousand words

gino
don't

jon
get the fuck out of my house

> *the sound of the internet*
> *the sound of flashing lights*
> *the sound of pictures being taken*
> *they appear*
> eduardo *and* mandy *sitting in a tree*
> dev *and* gino *in a boat*
> danny *and* jon – *prom king and queen at the dance*
> gino *and* eduardo *at an amusement park*
> danny *giving her valedictorian speech*
> mandy *at an archaeological dig*
> jon *in a football uniform*
> *an andy warhol print with the words*
> *i wonder if its possible to have a love affair that lasts forever*
> dev *getting a tattoo done*
> gino *on his hands and knees*

all
YOU DON'T LOOK AS DIFFERENT AS I THOUGHT YOU WOULD
'MEMBER WHEN I KISSED YOU JUST BECAUSE I COULD?
EVERYTHING STILL LOOKS THE SAME, IT FEELS THE SAME TO ME
MAYBE AFTER ALL THIS TIME I CANNOT TRUST MY MEMORY

SAME OLD CEILING, SAME OLD SHIRT YOU ALWAYS WEAR
NEVER BOUGHT A NEW ONE 'CAUSE YOU NEVER CARED
EVERYBODY KNOWS YOUR NAME 'CAUSE IT'S THE SAME ONE AS YOUR DADS
WE WERE TALKING SO MUCH SHIT, BUT THINGS WERE NEVER REALLY THAT BAD

AND IN BETWEEN THE LINES I GOT
THE COLOR OF, THE COLOR OF
THE MEMORY OF THE COLOR OF YOUR EYES
AND IN BETWEEN THE SIGHS I GOT
THE FEELIN OF THE FEELIN OF
THE MEMORY OF THE FEELING OF
THE MEMORY OF THE FEELING OF
THE MEMORY OF THE FEELING OF
THE MEMORY OF THE FEELING OF

SCENE

jon *leaves* danny *a message*

jon
hey babe
its me
jon
danny
i
i
i need to talk to you
there are some things i want to say
i want to say
i want to say
but every time i see you its like
the words
they disappear
youre the only person
the only thing
the only person ive ever been afraid of
afraid of
afraid of
afraid of losing
i want to be better
i want to be better
its just that
sometimes im afraid that by the time i figure out how
itll be too late
danny
danny
youre the best part of me
the thing i know ive done right
and i guess
i guess im afraid im bringing you down
and i haven't wanted to say that because
because its like once you say it you cant take it back you know
once you've said it
its too late
and i guess ive said it now
you intimidate me danny
i want to be as good for you as you are for me
and i wonder
i guess what im afraid of
danny
i guess what im afraid of
                    but its too late
        a loud beep as the message cuts off
            he doesn't know what to do...

SCENE

danny *and* mandy *eating burritos in* danny's *office*

danny
you have to
i insist

mandy
when did you start saying things like
"i insist"
you sound so old

danny
if the shoe fits

mandy
"if the shoe fits"
when did we become adults

danny
stop trying to change the subject

mandy
you don't think thatd be weird

danny
NO
take them
theyre already paid for
have fun
get away for a bit
take a vacation

mandy
come with me then

danny
i cant
i have things to take care of here

mandy
are you going to forgive him

danny
i don't know

mandy

id like to say im feeling more enlightened
but i still don't think i could

danny
this burrito is so good
i don't even care that im making a mess

mandy
that would be really big of you
if you could forgive him
i wish i could learn how

danny
its stupid
i never eat like this
afraid ill get fat
funny how concerned we are with physical weight
and yet none of us can let go of our emotional baggage
we hold grudges
we should forgive each other
that's got to be more important than not fitting into jeans right?

mandy
karmic fat
gross

danny
you know whats not gross?

mandy
what

danny
BURRITOS

SCENE

danny *stands at the door*
getting ready to come home to jon
bruise *appears in the distance singing a song*

bruise

YOU DON'T LOOK AS DIFFERENT AS I THOUGHT YOU WOULD
'MEMBER WHEN I KISSED YOU JUST BECAUSE I COULD?
EVERYTHING STILL LOOKS THE SAME, IT FEELS THE SAME TO ME
MAYBE AFTER ALL THIS TIME I CANNOT TRUST MY MEMORY

danny *is with* jon

danny

i have a confession
i don't see art when i look at the sky
i wikipedia things more than i should
im tone deaf
i wish i was kinder to myself
but i wish i was kinder to others even more
sometimes im a bad listener because im trying to think of the next thing im going
to say
im afraid ill sound stupid
a lot
i cheated in french class in high school and in college
sometimes i make up french sounding words in front of other people so i can look
smart
i wish i ate more cheese
i wish i could lounge around at home for days and not
Do
Anything
i have really bad taste in movies and i know it
i shake my head yes in agreement when i don't know what people are talking
about
i am afraid to reveal these things to anyone
but mostly to you

jon *begins to cry*

half the time
i feel like im broken
and i resent you for not looking at me
for not understanding me
when in reality i haven't let you by keeping so much of myself from you
i am a mess of contradictions and though i don't understand it
i do know one thing
i feel alright when im with you
imperfections and all
but i need you to feel the same way
so do you?

jon *gets up and kisses* danny

354

jon
youre everything ive ever wanted

danny
youre everything ive ever wanted too
flaws and all

jon
im not perfect

danny
i know

jon
i just need you to accept that

danny
youre a fixer upper

they kiss

<u>**SCENE**</u>

mandy *is digging a giant hole*
eduardo *arrives*
hes holding a tin box

eduardo
what are you doing

mandy
did you bring it

eduardo
yea
its right here

mandy
i think the hole is just the right size

eduardo
for what

mandy
our pasts

mandy pulls out the wedding dress shes been wearing
and throws it
into
the hole

mandy
my wedding dress
the engagement ring dev bought me
the ticket stub to the movie the day you and i broke up
love letters
things i need to leave behind
now you

eduardo *throws in the tin box*

eduardo
that's everything
everything i learned about myself in one tiny box

mandy
good
less baggage this way

she starts to close the hole

eduardo
what if someone digs this up

mandy
likely

someday
someone will
some curious person
dying to get her hands on history
dying to understand and to learn about things past
let them deal with it when they do

        the hole is closed

eduardo
so what now

      mandy *pulls out two plane tickets*

mandy
honey moon present from danny

eduardo
you can still use those

mandy
yes
two open-ended tickets
thinking about getting lost in new zealand
you should come with me

eduardo
i cant
im scared
change
ive never been to new Zealand
ive never been anywhere

mandy
first time for everything

gino *scans an old picture*

THE VOICE OF FACEBOOK
gino has uploaded a new picture
make new photo profile picture?
yes
crop
new profile picture updated

gino *updates his facebook status*

THE VOICE OF FACEBOOK
new status update

gino
gino is staring his past in the face
fuck you past
you cant hurt me anymore

THE VOICE OF FACEBOOK
new message received from dev barlow

dev *appears*

dev
i didn't think youd come to see me

gino
yea
well
somethings change
somethings don't
apparently im still a masochist

dev
youre a hard man to find
your profile pic

gino
im staring my past in the face

dev
it's a fucked up picture
you should change it

gino
i will
when i find something better

dev
you look good

gino
so do you
so you still come here huh
your sacred spot

dev
yea
it's the only place that reminds me of you

gino
so what do you want

dev
just wanted to know if we could hang out

gino
start where we left off
as if the last ten years hadn't happened
as if the world hadn't changed
you want to build a house on a fault line after an earth quakes occurred
and act like its still the same

dev
still thinking too far ahead i see

gino
it's a talent

                              dev *takes his shirt off*
gino
what are you doing?

dev
haven't actually been in the water since the last time we were together
thinking it's time

                    gino *notices the tattoo on* dev's *arm*
gino
what is that

dev
whats what

gino
on your arm

dev
it's a tattoo
a quote
from some artist
this guy i once loved told it to me

gino
i wonder if its possible to have a love affair that lasts forever

a breath
gino
that's my handwriting

dev
got it done the next day
so i wouldn't ever forget
like it

gino
who are you

dev
i don't know about forever
but theres planty of time to find out
hey

gino
what

dev
c'mere

gino
why

dev
just c'mere

gino
what are you doing

dev
take a picture with me

dev *takes out his blackberry*
or iPhone
who cares

dev pus his arm around *gino* and takes a picture of them

gino
what are you doing

dev
uploading it to facebook

THE VOICE OF FACEBOOK
new photo uploaded
make photo profile picture
yes
new profile picture updated

gino
its on the internet

dev
forever

gino
that means it's possible
                    dev takes off his pants
          socks
                boxer briefs
                        everything

dev
you see me
im only a man
made of flesh and blood
this is what i have to offer you
this body that wont last forever
the words i can form in my mouth
the thoughts i can conjure
i have love to give
and it has its limitations
but ill try
every day ill try to force them
that is the only promise i can make you

                dev howls in animalistic delight
                    like a man about to start a war

dev
you coming
                he runs into the water
                        gino stands there

gino
i have a secret

361

i am a masochist
i have hope
thatll ultimately destroy me
or get me real far
lets hope for the latter

and then eduardo *appears*

eduardo
gino
new zealand is like nothing ive ever seen before
there are endless rolling mountains that go for miles and miles
and sheep everywhere
ive never heard accents like these
im trying to articulate what im feeling
but im having a hard time
mandy and i are doing really well
she loves me
its such an odd feeling

mandy
and we finally had sex
tell him
tell him
i know you want to

eduardo
and it was
it felt tender
it felt like the most real thing ive ever done
i still haven't told her about you and dev
soon
we're going to armenia next
see where my dad grew up
see where it all started
the roots
i miss you
i feel like we spend a lot of time witht those three words
i miss you
i miss you
like two passing ships in the night
is that that saying
anyway
im running out of room on this card
youll come meet up with us soon wont you
i have so many thing to show you
so many things to tell you
the world here

it's a different
it's a different place
anyway
im sorry ill be missing the reunion
youll have to tell me all about it
is it true wilson chin got arrested for drugs
how did everyone turn out
okay-
lets skype soon
i know you hate it but i want to see your face
hear your voice
love
eddy
P S
I SEE YOU!

      and then he vanishes
        along with everything else

     end of play.

Made in the USA
Middletown, DE
08 October 2022

12315564R00217